CYN NO MORE

Lareesa Fonville Willis

Lareesa Fonville Willis

Fonville Publishing, P. O. Box 35893. Richmond, VA 23235

- Dedicated in Loving Memory -

To my father, Elder Lynwood E. Fonville, Sr. (1949-2005)

For teaching me how to persevere

To my grandmothers,

Mary S. Branch (1925-2008) & Marjorie L. Fonville (1928-1988)

For teaching me the power of prayer

To my grandfather, Herbert L. Branch (1925-1998)

For teaching me the value of hard work

This book is also dedicated to everyone who has a dream.

Never, ever give up.

"I can do all things through Christ which strengthens me." Phil 4:13

Lareesa Fonville Willis

Table of Contents

Lareesa Fonville Willis

Acknowledgments

First and foremost, I would like to thank God. Without Him, I am nothing. He is everything to me. My mother, Elder Katrina B. Fonville...Words cannot express how much I love you. Thank you for your unconditional love and support. You instilled in me that I can do everything through Christ who strengthens me... thank you, thank you, thank you! Monnie... I'll love you forever (4-5-8). My brothers, Donnell and Earl... Thank you for being the best big brothers a girl could have.

A big thank you to everyone who has supported and encouraged me, not only in the creation of this book, but also in my many other endeavors. I love you all.

Lareesa Fonville Willis

Chapter 1
Lost and Found

My eyes aren't willing to evade the image that is in my view. Although I'd seen her before, it was quite mysterious the way she walked into the library this rainy October night. It's about 7 o'clock and the classes at Thomas Jefferson High School down the street had recently begun. Hanging out at the library seems to be the new cool thing for teenagers to do. Internet access and the ability to peep through adult literature feed their raging hormones. They also love the recent coffeehouse addition to the top floor. Looks like one of those cafés you'd find at a ritzy bookstore.

My brain commands my eyes not to stare, but they won't listen. All black adorned her curvaceous body, as if in mourning. She wore a cashmere v-neck sweater, perfectly creased slacks, boots with a heel no less than three inches and carried some sort of designer handbag. Her dark brown, wavy hair added to her splendor. And, although her lips creasing upwards would add to the memory I was collecting, no smile shone on her wet face. She holds an umbrella, but she is soaking wet. The woman places her umbrella into the brass stand at the door. Her boots trail a couple of leaves from outdoors; one red, the other yellow. I nod hello, as I've done before, which is met with a half nod that advises me not to bother her. Her heels tap the concrete floor as she walks right past my desk and heads straight for the computers down the corridor. All of the ten mini cubicles are in use and it irritates her. She sits in a nearby chair, places her bag down, and attempts to wait until one is free. She makes a futile attempt to read a magazine, but throws it down seconds after picking it up off the coffee table. I can hear her sighs of impatience from where I stand at the information booth.

Minutes go by and her impatience grows. So much so, that she begins to shift in the brown leather chair. With her arms folded over her chest, her right leg starts to shake and she begins to bite the right corner of her lower lip. For a split second, I think I see a drop of blood. But, I blink and can't confirm it.

I walk over to her, my shoes clicking as my heels meet the floor with each step. I silently wish my size 11's won't be noticed as I awkwardly approached her. The sweet smell of her perfume meets me first. It's as if lavender and rose petals kissed the sun. It awakens senses in me that I've never known. I take a moment to inhale the aroma, letting it fill my lungs and warm my soul. Before I open my mouth to utter a sound, I swallow to make sure my vocal cords are well lubricated.

"Umm, excuse me, but I have a computer at my

desk you can use, if you like." She looks up at me and her brown eyes hold me, almost like a trance.

"Yes, I'd like that very much," she said. As she stands up and picks up her handbag, I notice it is a Gucci original. I'd admired one similar to it in a Vogue magazine a few weeks back. So much, in fact, that I cut the picture out and pressed it into the sticky pages of my dream book.

"Follow me," I said leading her to my workstation. The desk is a bit cluttered from the books, paper, pencils, and little white cards that are strewn about. She doesn't seem to mind and I smile, making sure I show no teeth. I tell her, "You can sit here," as I point to my wooden stool.

"Thanks," the woman said.

"Take all the time you need." I backed away to

give her a bit of privacy. She sits down, placing the handbag on the floor beside her, and begins to strike the keys of the computer keypad.

"I really appreciate this," she said turning her head towards me.

She looks at me as if for the first time, as if she just notices me. I feel her eyes summing me up, causing me to look away. I become even more self-conscience than I already am. Embarrassment sets in, caused by my Wal-Mart outfit and Payless shoes. *Surely, her clothing came from some fancy boutique*, I thought. I say a quick prayer that she won't notice the run in my pantyhose.

I tried to help the run by dabbing on clear nail polish this morning. I never wear polish on my nails, but my gold plated cross necklace received a few strokes. I can't afford the real gold necklace I'd seen at Jared's on Midlothian Turnpike, so I try to make my fake ones hold on to their color as long as possible. I put that in my dream book, too.

She can tell, I just know it, I thought, but she just turns back to the monitor without saying anything else, anxious to get online. I pretend to sort papers while attempting to get a glimpse of the website that is downloading.

It's Yahoo! I'd know that red letter logo anywhere. I practically live on the internet. Sometimes, I feel as if my online family cares about me more than my real-life family. I check my email before I check my voicemail, not that anyone calls anymore; except, of course, the occasional bill collector or two. I did, however, make friends with Brice, the collections supervisor who tried to get me to pay what I owed on my school loan. I made him feel so sorry for me one day, I guess, that he called me on his off time. I didn't mind him calling. It was nice to see a number on my caller ID, other than an 800 number. Eventually, we exchanged internet information, like email addresses and screen names and the rest is history, as they say.

She began typing her username and password and I didn't mean to glance and make a mental note of it, but I did. *Hmmm*, I thought to myself, *JessicaLuv313*. I wondered what the 313 meant. *A birthday perhaps*, which seems to be the numbers of choice when it comes to creating a login username. *Wouldn't that be a coincidence?* I thought. *My birthday is the thirteenth of March. No way this woman shares my astrological sign, let alone my day. A fish she definitely is not. We seem so different*, I thought, putting it out of my head.

I fiddle with folders in a file cabinet behind her as I try to see what she is reading but an old man comes up to the desk. I walk up to help him.

"May I help you, sir?"

He replies, "How do I check out this book?"

I point to Madge at the desk closer to the door, "If you have your ID, she can help you fill out a library card form."

The elderly gentleman walks away slowly, shifting his weight from one foot to the other, seemingly in pain. I thought of my grandfather, who passed away 6 years before. All the wisdom in the world left the day he took his last breath as far as I am concerned. Grandpa Manias loved me and I knew it from deep within my core. He understood me. Sometimes I feel as if he was the only one who did. I visit his gravesite often, making sure his flowers haven't blown away and the tombstone is clean. I talk to him sometimes and when the wind blows and hits my face I feel as if I've been kissed. I miss his whiskered salt and pepper mustache against my cheek as we said our hellos and our goodbyes. I was there as he left this world. I would've traded places if I could and tried to, but God didn't see fit to take me instead.

I watch Madge as she helps the old gentleman and feel wetness glide down my right cheek. I wipe it, not being phased by yet another tear.

The words "Are you ok?" interrupt my thoughts. For a moment, I'd forgotten about the beautiful woman at my desk. "Yes, I'm fine."

"Ok, good. I'm done" she said rushing. Thank you again for letting me use your computer."

"No problem." She is too busy leaving to hear me.

She picks up her umbrella from where she'd placed it about an hour before and walks out into the rain, which now had become only a drizzle. I watch her leave, just as I'd watched her enter and for a split second, wish I was her. I wondered, *where is she rushing off to? Who is waiting for her? What kind of life does she lead?* It had to be more interesting than mine. I'm practically nonexistent to the real world.

Viewing my surroundings, I begin to get ill. "I'm sick of this place," I say, not realizing I'd spoken the words aloud. The smell of stale pages and dusty wood make my nostrils burn. I've worked here for fourteen years and I'm sick of books. Fiction and non-fiction alike, I want my own story to tell. This is where people come to get their share of history or their fill of imaginary people, places, and things. For the first time, I feel trapped by words. I'm stuck within sentences that have no punctuation.

Looking up at the clock, the little hand fingered the eight and the big hand nudged the nine. Only fifteen minutes till closing time, and I can't muster the energy to clean up my desk.

I do, however, make my way over to the computer to shut it down. It is then that I notice the woman had left her purse.

Glancing quickly around the room, I look to see if she is returning for her handbag, but she is nowhere in sight. Then, I look to see if anyone is watching me. *Is anyone watching me? Wait, what am I thinking? I'm not a thief.* I have to turn this into lost and found. Just like I did with the wallet that had three hundred dollars in it over by the old card catalog section last month. I could've really used that money. But, I did the right thing and turned it in.

Although I had admired the bag on models, I didn't want to steal the pocketbook. But, I am curious. I am curious to see what is inside this mystery woman's

19

purse. I am curious to see how it will look on my shoulder. *I'll just borrow it for the night*, I thought.

The last of the patrons gather their belongings and exit the building. Madge and a security guard, Tony, are waiting up by the glass doors for me. Madge is a pretty cool person to work with, just extremely nosey. Tony is as gay as they come. He doesn't take any mess from anybody. He thinks he's so fierce, switching up and down the book filled aisles. I hate to admit it, but he is.

We usually walk out to our cars together because Broad Street has seen its share of violence and tonight is no different. Hurriedly, I place the woman's purse in my grocery bag, under the Cream of Wheat I purchased during my lunch break from the corner market. Shutting down the computer, I gather the rest of my belongings, and head for the door. I think, *surely the woman will be back tomorrow looking for it*. I feel guilty as

I walk past Tony and Madge. "See you guys tomorrow," I say while rushing off to my gray Ford Taurus. I place the key in the ignition and think to myself, *I can't wait to get home.*

Lareesa Fonville Willis

Chapter 2
Who's There?

The drive home isn't that long. Once I take I-95
to Chippenham Parkway, I'm there in about 15
minutes, despite the wet roads. Cold Harbor Manor is
where I call home. The apartment community mostly
consists of older people, although a few young couples
live nearby. It's quiet here.

Sometimes it can be a little too quiet. An
occasional ambulance siren can be heard because of the
hospital close by, but other than that, nothing. There
are lots of trees and boulders which make it resemble a
park.

As I make my way up the stairway to apartment

#9B, I feel as if I'm being watched. I look around and notice nothing out of the ordinary and continue up the stairs. I unlock the door and enter my 2-bedroom apartment. My Pomeranian, Lucy, greets me at the door, with her tail wagging excitedly.

"I'll take you out in a minute," I say to her as I close the door and walk over to the sofa to put my bags down. I knew I was pushing it since she'd been inside all day, but I still ask, "Can you hold it?"

She scampers to the door looking back at me, then back to the door. I ignore her and begin to carefully remove the handbag from the brown paper grocery bag. I'm in awe. The purse is even more gorgeous than in the advertisements. It is a medium sized, black leather bag with double handles and a snap closure. It has fringes with bamboo detail and most of all, it has an authentic Gucci logo engraved on it! I can't stop staring at this bag. It is worth at least two thousand dollars, more than my entire wardrobe, including shoes.

What exactly my intentions are with the bag, are unbeknownst to me at this moment. One part of me, wants to keep the bag because I've never owned anything so lovely. Another part, wants to locate the woman and give her back the bag, as an excuse to meet her again. *Maybe we'll become friends*, I think. *Naaaa*. As quickly as the thought comes to mind, I push it out. *She'll never want to hang out with someone like me.*

My staring continues until it is interrupted by the streaming sound of urine being discharged on the tile at the front door.

"Lucy," I scream! I scare her and she runs from the accident scene tracking little paw prints of pee from the tile to the carpet.

I don't want to place the mystery bag down, but

I don't want my small apartment to smell of pungent urine either. Sitting the bag down on the glass coffee table as if it were a jewel, I get the pine cleaner and begin cleaning up the mess. Remembering the funny feeling I had coming up the stairs, relief comes over me when I realize I don't have to go back outside tonight.

"Thank you, Lucy." She hears her name, appears from behind the kitchen wall, and comes to me slowly. "It's Ok, it was my fault." I rub her head and she loves me back by licking my arm.

"Come on Lucy, let's go see what's inside this bag." I sit my round behind back on the couch and finally open the bag. Inside are the following contents: a matching Gucci wallet, a pale green tube of lipstick, black eyeliner, comb, journal, cell phone, sealed envelope, and a small glass bottle of perfume, called Monree. I open the wallet to find a Virginia Driver's License, 2 credit cards, a picture of the woman with a man, and a Kroger plus card.

Even in a picture taken by the Department of Motor Vehicles, she embodies the word feminine. *We have similar features*, I think. *Well, we would if I lost some of this weight.* I look down at myself and back again at the picture, shaking my head. *Why can't I be more like her?*

Her name is Jessica Persugla. I wonder, *where are her ancestors from with a name like that? At least it is unique. Not like mine, Evans.*

Cynthia Renee Evans is on my birth certificate, but people have called me Cyn for so long, I think its been changed permanently. My mama, Rozella Mae, never married my daddy. Although, I was told he proposed marriage several times. Rodney Lee Boyd loved him some Zella. He would say, "That's my Zella." That is, when he was sober. Without the clear liquid he would buy from Mr. Joe up on Q Street in

Churchill, he was a good man. But, once he got that Mason jar poison in his blood, it was all ova.

They courted for about two years before they moved in together. Both families disapproved of their living arrangement, but they did it anyway. Mama loved him so much. He was from a good Christian family, handsome, and all the ladies were jealous because she snagged him. Everything was going good between them, until early one morning; daddy came home drunk and wanted to have sex with mama. She never liked the smell of booze on his breath, but tolerated it because he was such a good catch.

One particular morning, daddy came home so drunk that he didn't look like himself. She had never seen him that drunk and the stench made her stomach turn. She said it looked as if he was demon possessed, with fire in his eyes. He wanted to have sex, but she told him no and tried to put him to bed. Daddy didn't take no for an answer and instead forced her on the bed and raped my mama. She says she has two things to always remind her of that day: a scar on the left side of her face and me.

I don't remember the first time I was called Cyn. Knowing mama, it probably started when I was still in the womb. Mama says she calls me Cyn because I am the product of their sin. My name is a constant reminder that I'm her shame. She told me once that she regret they day I was born. She says I'm the reason why daddy left her.

Daddy left us before I was born. Ms. Pearl, the lady who sat on the stoop outside my apartment growing up, said that daddy left mama for some fast talkin' and slick walkin' woman named Yolanda. I was under the steps collecting cans to recycle and overheard her talking. I never knew who Yolanda was. But at far as I was concerned, she could have him. I didn't need

29

Lareesa Fonville Willis

an alcoholic rapist as a father.

Chapter 3
Leave a Message

Placing the contents back inside the purse, I

sigh, stand up, and take the grocery bag into the

kitchen. While putting the cereal box into the cabinet, I

think *Jessica probably has noticed by now that it's gone.* I place

some dry dog food into Lucy's bowl and open the

refrigerator door. The cold air sends a chill through me.

Chinese leftovers are in my view and I place a half-

eaten container of shrimp fried rice and gravy into the

microwave, making sure I remove the metal handle

first. *Three minutes should do it*, I figure. I set the timer and

head back into the living room to feed my tropical fish.

About fourteen flakes or so go into water and I watch

them greedily eat every morsel as if I won't be back

tomorrow to give them more.

31

BEEP! The microwave is loud and startles me for a moment. I turn and head back into the small kitchen area. Grabbing a plastic fork, I stir my dinner and head back to the living room to eat on the sofa. I snatch the remote from the coffee table and turn on the television. It is shortly after eleven o'clock and the TV show, Will and Grace, is on. I love this show, although I can't admit that to everyone. My mother would have a conniption if she knew I liked watching a show involving gay people. I can identify with Jack in some ways. He just wants to be loved and accepted for the person he is, without regrets. I wish some of his traits would rub off on me. *I need his confidence.*

My leftovers are not good at all. The fried rice is hard and the shrimp is rubbery. *Perhaps three minutes was too long, oh well.* I wasn't supposed to be eating this anyway. I keep saying I'm going to eat healthier. *Well, I did get the cereal today.*

The sweet sound of a jazz band fills the room, surprising me. *Where is this noise coming from?* I look up at the television, but then notice the noise is coming from the cell phone in the purse. I contemplate answering it for a moment, and then decide against it.

It stops ringing and a few moments later, an all too familiar ring alerts me the caller has left some sort of message. Curious, I grab and open the flip phone to find that a voice message was left. Realizing the phone's carrier, I smile. I've owned this type of phone for years, despite the outrageous pricing plans. With the phone in my right hand, I become conscious to the fact that most of these phones allow you to press 1 + Talk to check your voicemail. I was about to find out if she had hers set up the same way. Hesitantly, I press the number 1 and the green talk button with my right thumb nail. Almost instantaneously, her phone number appears and connects me to her private voicemail.

I fear this is an invasion of privacy. I should hang up now, but I hear:

"18 Saved messages. 1 New message. Main menu. To listen to your messages, press 1. To send a message, press 2. To change your personal options, press 3. To exit press star-."

I should definitely hang up. I wouldn't want anyone listening to my personal messages. Well, that wouldn't happen because nobody really calls me anymore. Instead, I get emails, which I just remember I hadn't checked yet.

"To listen to your messages press…"

I can't stop now. I'm too curious as to who was calling and why. I press 1 on the phone's keypad and hear:

"First new message, from phone number 8-0-4-5-5-5-1-2-3-2, Received October 12th at 11:47pm. Hey sexy, this is Des. Thought you were going to call me so we could hook up tonight. I can't wait to finally meet you and do all the things we've talked about. I dreamt about the picture you sent me the other day. I know you said it was an old picture, but I'm sure you didn't change that much. I'll tell you bout the dream later. I'm sure you're worth it, but don't keep me waiting. I'm staying at Inntown Suites on Robius Road. I'm in Room #119. I'm hard, just for you. Bye."

Just like on my phone, I press four to repeat the message to make sure what I'd just heard was real. It was. *Oh my God. Did he say he was hard?*

Oh my… I need to hang up.

"Fist saved message."

"Jessica, honey, its mom. Call me, I'm worried about you. I love you."

If I didn't know better, I'd swear that voice sounded just like ...

"Next message."

"Hi beautiful, thank you for letting me hold you again last night. You felt like silk. I wanted to cook you breakfast but you left so suddenly. No goodbye. No nothing. What gives?"

Hold up. That was a woman's voice....

"Next message."

"Jessica thanks for putting a smile on my face. I

guess Virginia is for lovers. I'll call you when I'm in town again. My wife is going to a conference week after next. Be ready. Hey, what am I saying? You always are. Bye sweetie."

Married men? What the...

"Next message."

"This is an automated call from Walgreen's pharmacy. Your prescription is ready for pick up at the following location: 56340 Buford Road. Please stop by within 3 days of this notification or your prescription will be added back into our inventory. Thank you for shopping at Walgreen's pharmacy."

She didn't look sick....

"Next message."

"Honey it's me again. I'm worried sick. Please call me. I won't hound you about the church. I just want to know that you are ok."

Again, that voice…

"Next message."

"Hey baby, I'll be returning from Japan on the 14th. I want to see you baby, all of you. Call me, you know the number."

Oh Lawd, she's an international whore…

"Next message."

"Hey, this is Larry. I'll be coming your way next weekend. If you're not busy, maybe we can meet up like last time. Let me know. Maybe I can get our same room. My new cell number is 555-6000."

"Next message."

"Jess, it's me. Don't forget our lunch plans today at The Croaker Spot. The reservations have already been made. I'll meet you there at…"

KNOCK! KNOCK! KNOCK! Startled, I drop the phone causing it to close and hang up. *Jesus!* Grandpa Manias always said to call on Him in times of trouble. I hope the thought of him will help because my mouth wouldn't utter a sound. I look across the room at the wall clock hanging over the computer. It clearly reads 11:56pm. *Who could that be at this hour?* Lucy barks one time and stares at the door. I don't move, and even though my heart beats faster, my breathing slows. This is Richmond and I don't open my door for anybody after dark.

A small part of me wants to muster the courage

to go to the door and look out the peephole to see who it is. However, my body is frozen like ice and sticks to the pleather sofa. Even though this is a good neighborhood, I hate living here by myself. Everyone sees when I leave and is aware of when I get home. I've got to change my schedule up a bit. Note to self: *get an alarm system.*

The knocking begins again, this time firmer. *Why aren't they using the doorbell?* I look down at Lucy who looks just as scared as I am. I wait a few minutes and hear nothing further. I assume they are gone when Lucy utters a low half bark and lies down. *Humph, some dog I have.*

Chapter 4
Risky Business

I pick the cell phone up off the floor and place it on the coffee table, still processing the information I'd heard on her voicemail. *Is she a prostitute or just promiscuous?* I ask myself. Not that promiscuity should be taken lightly these days. Diseases are out there. From looking at her, I saw sophistication.

Not a hint of what I call "slutitis."

Slutitis {sluht – eye – tis} N. A condition which results from giving up the "goods" too many times to undeserving individuals to whom one has not entered into marriage with.

Goods {goo ds} N. Refers to sexual favors or acts, see also goodies.

Forget Webster's dictionary. I have my own.

Something inside of me is still intrigued by this woman. I can't put my finger on it, but I want to know more. I should prepare myself to return the items to the owner, but instead I reach for the journal. From the looks of it, it's well used. Some pages are torn and creases are abundant. Part of the back cover is torn near the bottom and some pages look as if they had previously been wet, perhaps by tears. I open the mauve cloth cover to discover the following words:

If you are reading this, I am more than likely dead. But, on the off chance that I'm still alive and you've found this, please return it. My life's story lies between these pages. If you must rape these pages with your eyes, do so at your own risk.

Jessica Lyn Persugla

254 Revelation Lane

Richmond, VA 23225

Whoa. Do so at my risk, huh? This journal is too small to hold a whole life story. Humph. There couldn't be more than 100 to 150 little pages here and its only half way full. I turn the page.

March 18th

I received this journal in the mail today. I got it off of eBay just to get my feedback score up a little. It only cost a buck. I don't think I'm going to use it much. We'll see. I used to keep a journal when I was younger, but I lost it when they made me move here from Kinston, NC eight years ago. When my mom, Jo, died my life changed. I found out that Jo was really my aunt, that my real mom was alive, and that I had a sister.

43

March 19th

I'm back. I'm having problems with my car, so I had to ride the bus downtown today. I saw her.

March 20th

Jim and I fought again today. He just doesn't understand me. He wants me to be this perfect little Susie Homemaker type, but I ain't the one. Especially if he won't...

March 21st

This Puerto Rican dude I met off the net took me out tonight. We only went to Applejack's, but it was still nice. His picture looked better than he did, but

I still did him. After all, he did buy me country fried

steak. Oh wait, I paid the check, because he forgot his wallet at home. He promised to mail me the money tomorrow. His breath stunk but I didn't care. He wanted me, even if it was only for one night. Somebody wanted me.

March 23rd

I was sick as a dog yesterday. I spent half the day in the bathroom and the other half in bed. Today I am regrouping. I need to figure out this thing I call my life.

March 24th

He called today…

I continued reading and felt like I was starting to know this woman better than I knew myself. Without realizing it, my eyes close and my thoughts dominate my subconscious and turns into a dream.

A woman dressed in black leather with a mask over her face led me down a long red painted hallway. To a door…a black door, even the knob. Inside was a room so white it blinded me. I wanted to put shades on, but I had none. So I covered my eyes with my left hand, peering through my fingers. I briefly see a figure of a man with rays around him, shining like the sun. I can hardly see. I take a step toward the light, but he becomes further away. Squinting, I try to catch a glimpse of the light source. Taking another step, I hold my right hand out. The light is dense, almost tangible. My hand is heavy in the air, but my body feels light. I need to see…

Chapter 5
The Lie Begins

RING! RING! I abruptly awaken to the loud ringing of my house telephone. I sit up causing the journal to fall between the sofa cushions and my head to throb. I locate the phone, first with my eyes, then with my hands, desperate to quiet the noise.

I sleepily say, "Hello?" and then let out a loud yawn.

"Cyn, where are you?" a female asks.

I recognize Madge's voice and clear my throat.

"Cyn? You're late. I can't cover for you all day,

you know."

I look at the clock, its 11:12am. *Oh snap!*

"Oh, I'm so sorry Madge. I must've overslept."

"Well get it together girl and get down here. This woman was waiting here this morning when we opened the doors. She says she left her purse at your station last night. I told her there was no purse turned in to lost and found. She swears up and down that she left it. Did you see a purse?" she said all in the same breath.

My mind blanks for a second. *Shoot! I should have gotten up early this morning and snuck it back in!*

"No, I didn't see a purse," I lie. *Oh My God, I'm going to hell. I'm a thief and a liar.*

"I knew the chick was crazy. Get here when you can girl," she says.

"I will. Bye."

"Bye."

I hang up the phone, stand up, and head for the bathroom. Ignoring the toilet, I turn my attention to the shower. I turn the water on, first the hot, then the cold making sure the temperature is just right. Noticing I still have on what I wore to work yesterday, I strip. Starting with the blouse and bra; then the skirt, pantyhose, and undies followed, hitting the floor in one swoop. I take a second to look in the mirror, but am immediately disgusted by the sight. "You've got to lose this weight," I tell myself. Grabbing a hair clip off the bathroom sink, I pin up my shoulder length brown hair. I begin to step over the pile of clothes I'd just put on the floor, and then decide to just kick them closer to the wall. I make my way into the streaming waterfall and close the plastic liner. I notice some mildew stains near the bottom. *It's time to throw this thing away.*

I exhale, allowing the water to relax me. Grasping my sponge, I squeeze entirely too much shower gel on it on purpose. *Mmmm, I love a good lather.* I inhale, allowing the scent of pure rain to intoxicate my senses. The fragrant, luxurious lather swirls across my large wet frame and I forget that

I'm late for work. I feel beautiful at this moment. The shower is my man and he is telling me with his steam that I am wanted. I need to be purified, cleansed. I let him explore every crevice without hesitation. I pull down the shower head, turn the stream to pulsate, and allow my cave to be entered. No longer in hibernation, I let out a sigh, then a moan. The vibrations I feel cause me to lean against the wall, opening my legs further. My inner walls catch every pulsating drop and a competition then begins; my faucet against his.

Afterwards, no time for a cigarette even if I did smoke. I finish washing, rinse, shut off my man, and step out of the tub. The tile floor stubbornly receives the drops of water that drip off my now moisturized skin. A towel eager to soak up the wet beads hangs on the back of the door. A white terry cloth robe hangs adjacent to it. I opted for the towel although I would love nothing more than to stay home, lounge around in the robe, and fix some of the Cream of Wheat I'd brought yesterday. Breakfast is a rare treat. *I'm off the next few days. I'll have time for breakfast then.*

Once dry, I head to the bedroom closet to pick out my clothes. Nothing fancy; a blue and black top with the same black slacks I'd worn three days prior. It's hanging up, but I smell the crotch anyway. Smells like FDS, *I'm good to go.*

Walking over to the dresser, I put on deodorant, and grab my under garments from the top drawer. I dress, remove the clip from my hair, comb it without looking, and lotion my face, hands, and elbows. I head back to the bathroom to brush my teeth. The ritual of whether I get spit diluted toothpaste on my clothing tells me if I'm going to have a good or bad day.

Ahhh, no stains, it's going to be a good day. I head towards the living room, put on my shoes, and prepare to walk Lucy. She excitedly knows the routine and beats me to the door. I hook the leash to her pink collar and off we go. She did her business in record time and seemed content with staying home alone again. I lock the door and head to work, still late.

Chapter 6
The Scent

"G-L-A-M-O-R-OU-S." The voice of a pop singer spills into the car. "If you ain't got no money take yo broke a—home," the radio blares.

"I guess I better turn around and go home," I say aloud for the insides of my Taurus to hear. I sing and drive along wishing that I, too, could live the glamorous life.

At work, I arrive to find an arm crossed Jessica sitting near my work station waiting for me. *Dang!* I pretend I don't see her and stop to speak to

Madge to buy me a little time to get my lie

straight.

"I made it," I say to Madge.

"I see. It's about time." She points and rolls her eyes at Jessica. "That chick came back and said she wasn't leaving till you got here."

So much for buying me time. I turn towards my station and approach an anxious Jessica.

"Where is it?" she asks, looking me straight in the eyes.

"Where is what?" I say, laying my keys down, pretending I hadn't the slightest clue what she is talking about.

"You know exactly what I'm talking about. My handbag," she said agitated. "I left it here last night while I was using your computer." She gestures towards

the monitor and keyboard.

"Are you sure? I didn't see any bag." I begin

looking around as if I were really looking for

something.

"Don't play me Cyn," she says.

She catches me off guard by saying my name.

My library name tag and name plate only has Ms. Evans

on it. *How did she know my name?* I couldn't answer.

"Look," she says trying to be calm. "I know you have

my belongings. I couldn't have possibly left them

anywhere else. You can play stupid all you want with

your little co-workers. But, I need my stuff back."

I swallow, not able to speak. I look around to

see if anyone is witnessing this. Madge, of course, is

stuck to the scene like glue. *Nosey heffa!*

All she needed was popcorn to enjoy the show. "And, I'm 'gonna get it one way or the other," Jessica states.

"Are you threatening me?" I asked.

"Threatening you?" She let out a sarcastic chuckle and I couldn't help but to notice how even more beautiful she looked. *I want to be this beautiful.*

Why can't I be this beautiful? She leaned in close to me so I could only hear her say, "I am going to say this one last time. I want my bag back and every single item inside. If so much as a piece of lint is removed, you will have hell to pay." I heard her, but her closeness was more than I could bear. Her breath lingers on my skin and I feel numb. My nipples harden, even though there isn't the slightest breeze felt in the building.

She reaches in her pocket and hands me a business card with her perfectly manicured hands. "Give me a call later so I can pick it up," she says.

"I – I don't have your belongings," I stutter.

"Give-me-a-call-later-so-I-can-pick-it-up," she repeats slowly. Then she turns and walks out of the library. I feel strange like I'm watching a movie scene, but I can still smell her scent, making her presence real.

Lareesa Fonville Willis

Chapter 7
The Real L Word

Madge can't help herself. She hurriedly walks over to me cutting through the tantalizing aroma. *Dang!.* Another smell takes its place and I immediately became nauseous. In the three years we've worked together, I'd never noticed the disgusting stench of cigarettes coming from her before. *Ughhh!*

I twinkle my now itching nose as if I'm Samantha from the television show, *Bewitched.* "You ok?" she says, acting genuinely concerned, but I knew she was just being her usual nosey self.

I act as if I don't hear her. "What did she

whisper to you?"

"Nothing," I say moving over to my computer to finally log in.

Madge slid sideways in front of the pc. "I saw her whisper something to you. She was awful mad, girl. Tell me."

I can't stand this smoke smell. I make a face like she'd just farted and say, "Ewww, when did you start smoking?" trying to change the subject.

She backs up a little and says, "I just had a couple last night and this morning." She then lifts her shirt towards her nose, sniffs, and shrugs off the notion that she just might stink.

"Oh yeah? All these years, I've never known you to smoke," I questioned her.

"I used to smoke a long time ago. I stopped after my Dad-," she paused, "you know— but anyway, I met this guy last night at the Lights Bar down in Shockoe Bottom. Girrllll. He poooot it owne me!"

I start laughing, partly because she is so silly and also because that was the worst Jamaican accent I'd ever heard.

"Girl, you didn't?!" I ask, knowing full well she did.

"Oh, Yes I did! My body needed it! And if I didn't, my coochie woulda been mad at me forever!" She said, not caring that she was loud.

I hear a few sshhh's coming from the patrons in the background and tell Madge to keep it down with a hand gesture. She calls herself lowering her voice, but she really doesn't. She's too excited.

"He's sooo smooth, girl. Tall, built, and he's got the sexiest dimples." She looks around, pretending like she cares who hears her now and says, "On both cheeks!" She giggles like a school girl with a crush.

"You are so silly," I say, laughing at her.

"And, he's got pretty teeth!" She said, adding to her excitement.

"Pretty teeth?" I ask.

"Yeah, girl. You remember that blind date I had with that dude with no grill? You know, the one when he opened his mouth, I thought I was on candid camera?"

"Oh yeah. I remember," I say, only kind of

remembering.

"He was a hot mess. But this one, girlllllll!" Madge can hardly contain herself.

I look at her waiting for the rest of what she has to say.

"We talked for hours in the bar. He bought my drinks and listened to every word I said. He was even leaning in while I was talking." She looks in the air like she could see her thoughts. "That means he was genuinely interested in what I was saying!" She looks back at me.

"Uh huh," I say while I finish logging in and pull up my email.

"We have so much in common. He's not like the others. I know it's too soon, but I think I'm in love!”

Did this heffa just say she is in love? No freakin way. She really needs to stop confusing lust with love. This is about the fifth time she's "been in love" this year!

She doesn't wait for a response. "And guess what his name is? Mark!" She answers without taking a breath or before I could say 'what'. "We're M&M…like the candy…isn't that cute?"

She can't be serious. I smile like it's the cutest thing this side of heaven, hoping she'd forgotten why she came over here in the first place.

"I was in a good mood. Then that chick came in bringing down my high."

Dang, she didn't forget! I look back down at my computer.

"I was being nice till she looked me up and down like I wasn't worth 'nothin. I can't stand when people act like they 'betta than you." She rolls her eyes at nobody in particular and then continues talking. "And, looking all around behind the stations like she owned the place, even mine! We need security up in this piece during the day too! Tony woulda been all on her stuck-up behind."

"Yeah, we do," I agree, glancing at the cartful of books I need to reshelf.

"Look at all this, let me get to work. And, you...," I say being glad I just saw a patron at Madge's desk, "need to go and help that lady," I say pointing Madge sighs and walks away towards her desk to assist the woman. It was then that I realized she had on the same outfit she did yesterday.

"Humph," I say under my breath, wishing it were me who'd gotten lucky last night.

Chapter 8
The Keys

I finish my workday trying to put out of my mind what happened earlier with Jessica. The day went by seemingly fast and it was nine o' clock before I knew it. I notice Madge rushing to get her belongings together. *She's probably going to see the dude from last night.* I jealously roll my eyes at the thought, log out, and shut down my computer.

Tony called in sick, so he isn't here to walk us out. His usual replacement is Joe, a middle aged, white man with fine, salt and pepper hair. Mostly salt. He has gray eyes that are covered by glasses, with clear frames.

67

His face is aged, wrinkled by the years, I imagine; especially around the eyes. His pink lips are dry, cracked and peeling. *Some lip balm would do him a world of good*, I thought. His blue uniform is slightly baggy at the waist as if he'd lost some weight recently. His black shoes are unusually dusty, with one shoe lace partially untied. His high-water pants reveal a few inches of the dingy white socks he is wearing.

Joe moves to open the door for a woman walking with a cane and my eyes follow the jingling sound of his keys. There seems to be at least 30 keys hanging from his belt. As the woman exited the building, I watch as his eyes followed her and lingered a little too long. After her disappearance, he returned to his normal stance, looking off into space.

Joe doesn't really talk to any of the staff, except for his brief exchanges with Madge. But, then again, she makes people talk to her. Everyone else gets the occasional head nod or some sort of hand gesture. The only sounds I ever hear from him are from his coughs or when he clears phlegm from his throat. He carries a white handkerchief in his left pants pocket. He can be seen wiping his brow and mouth with it several times a day. Distancing himself from others, Joe seems to live in a world outside our own. It's as if he is just going through the motions of life. For a brief moment, I wonder what his story is, but I need to get home.

Madge says a rushed goodbye and heads towards her pickup truck. I manage to smile, say goodnight, and head in the direction of my vehicle. Reaching into my right jacket pocket, I feel an old candy wrapper, a near empty tube of lip balm, and some lint.

"Oh no," I huff. I reach into my left pocket, already knowing full well what I'd done. My keys are still on top of my desk, near the fake hibiscus plant.

Dang! I close my eyes in disbelief for a second, then sigh, turn around, and walk back toward the building. I look over to see if Madge is still around, but can only smell the fumes of her old, beat up truck. Normally, her truck has trouble starting or needs to be warmed up for at least five minutes before she can even think of putting it in gear. *That must've been some good...*

"Hey there, sweet thang," a voice comes out of nowhere startling me, interrupting my thoughts. I turn and my nose identifies the voice's owner before my eyes can. It's Mickey, the neighborhood drunk. I attempt to rub the stench of underarm funk and beer from my nostrils in one quick move.

Ugghhh! He's usually only around during the day begging for spare change from the library visitors. Annoyed, I turn back toward the building. Without acknowledging him, I continue walking up the ramp to the front entrance.

The lights are on, which doesn't mean anything considering they are left on 24 hours a day. Feeling my eyes fill up with liquid, I try the door handle hoping it will magically open. *No magic.* An intense feeling of panic comes over me when I realize I don't have the slightest idea what I am going to do. My car and apartment keys are locked inside of a building that won't open again until 8am in the morning. It's dark, getting cold, I suddenly have to pee, and a bum is somewhere behind me thinking I'm his sweet thing. I try the handle again, this time praying.

Dear God, I know I don't come to you often, but I need you...

"Are you ok, Ms. Evans?" a scratchy voice asks. It's Joe, the security guard! *I didn't even know he knew my name.* I almost jump into his arms, but control myself. I let out the biggest "Thank God" I could muster.

"No, I'm not alright. I've left my keys on my desk," I tell him.

He looks around as if he is looking for someone.

"Can you help me?" I ask.

His gaze turns to me and looks me straight in the eyes and gives me a devilish smile.

"Well, can you help me?" I ask again. "Don't you have keys to the building?"

"Why, yes ma'am. I would be glad to help you," he says with no emotion, beginning to look around again.

"Are you waiting on a ride or something?" I ask

him, wondering why he hasn't begun unlocking the door.

He looks back in my direction, but his eyes land on my chest. He says, "No, ma'am."

"Ooooohk," I say, getting nervous again. "It won't take but a minute to run in and grab my keys," I say turning my attention towards the door, then back to him.

He looks into my eyes, but says nothing. My heart starts beating faster.

"Listen, Joe," I ask, "Are you going to let me in the building or not?"

"Yes, ma'am," he replies, "I think I am."

"You think you are?" I question him, confused

at his response.

"Yes, ma'am," he says, still showing no emotion.

This ma'am thing is getting on my nerves and so is he. This is too spooky. *Dangit! Why did I have to forget my keys? I always put them in my pocket. They are always in my right pocket. If it weren't for that Jessica this morning, they would've been in my pocket!* My thoughts screamed inside my head.

"Joe, unlock the door please," I petition.

"I will, ma'am," he responded, this time smiling.

"When Joe? When will you open the door?" I ask as calmly as possible.

"I don't know yet," he says and scratches his

head.

This can't be happening. Why is this man playing games with me? What did I ever do to him?

"Joe, I really don't have a lot of time. I have people waiting on me," I lie.

He looks at me as if he knows I'm lying.

"No ma'am, you don't," he says smiling again.

"Yes, I do. I'm late for a party," trying my best to make it sound legit.

"I know something you don't know," he sings.

Oh my freaking God! This is a scene straight out of a movie! I refuse to be a victim and I take a step back from Joe, making room to run if need be. His smile turns into an all-out grin as if the game just started for him.

"How bad do you want those keys?" He asks.

"Excuse me?" I question him, not believing what he'd just asked.

"I said, how bad do you want those keys?" He asked again, still smiling.

I turn looking for someone, anyone. But I don't see anyone in sight, not even the drunk, Mickey.

"Look Joe, I don't want any trouble," I say putting my hands up between us, making it easier for me to make a fist.

Chapter 9
I Remember

I wake up in my bed, naked as usual, under a white flat sheet and my favorite comforter with a terrible headache. *Owww!* The pounding feels like my thoughts are trying to escape. I wish I could perform surgery right now and let them spill out onto the pillow. I try to pick my head up but it hurts so bad that I remain horizontal. It is light outside. I can tell from the rays of sun peering through the blinds covering the bedroom window. My eyes have trouble focusing, but I try to take a quick look at the digital clock on the wood nightstand. The red letters read 9:23. I close my eyelids again until my eyes and head can agree to work

77

together. I attempt to sit up again, this time succeeding. My right hand holds up my head, keeping it from being detached, I believe.

"Aspirin, I need aspirin," I say aloud in a whisper and Lucy appears wagging her tail. I stumble to the bathroom medicine cabinet to find my cure. My hands are shaking, but I manage to take three with no water and place the half empty bottle back in the mirrored cabinet. My eyes make out an image of myself in the mirror. Red eyes and a bruise on the right side of my head are staring at me. *What happened to me?* I think, causing my head to pound more. *Did I fall or something?* Wanting to lay back down, I head back to the bedroom. Once back inside the room, I notice my closet door is open.

What in the world? I stop, knowing full well that I never go to sleep without closing it. I've done so since I was a child. *Somebody's been here.*

I used to hide in closets when I was younger. Hide and Go Seek was my favorite game. Mama rarely played the game with me though. She would only tell me to hide when she had company over. Mostly, I played with Jazmine, my imaginary friend. She never could find me.

One day, mama went to the store and left her new friend, Manny, at the house watching a basketball game. I was hiding in the closet and he found me.

"Gotcha!" He said as his large frame towered over my seven-year-old body. "Let's play another game" he suggested, smiling. I liked playing games, but something deep inside me told me that I didn't want to play any of his. "Let's play husband and wife," he said. My eyes are wide and face frozen. Mama will be home soon. *Tell him that mama will be home soon!* My young mind pleads with my mouth, but I can't say anything. I'm scared.

He tries to grab me out of the closet.

"No, mister! I don't want to play this game!" I scream.

"Oh, you don't want to come out? That's ok, I'll come in." He said and made himself fit in the closet with me. He hovered over me and I had no way of escaping.

"Please, Mr. Manny. I don't want to play…" I pleaded.

"Shut up!" He yelled. "You're a tease just like your mama. His big hands shoved my dress up and pulled my panties down.

I screamed and cried for my mama and he slapped me, hard.

"You better shut up or when your mama comes home, I'm going to kill her."

My screams stopped in my throat. I was now shaking.

"You walk 'round here, in these short, little dresses showing your legs. You know you want it, pretty girl." He said, unzipping his pants with one hand and holding me down with the other. The words 'pretty girl' rang in my ears. I close my eyes tight and wished I was invisible, like Jazmine.

"I know how y'all like it," he said, pulling my legs apart.

I didn't fully understand what was happening then. All I knew was that my young body ripped with pain and when he left, I couldn't move. When mama came home, Manny was gone. She blamed me for making him leave, too. *Closets are not my friend.*

I look around, trying to notice if anything else is out of place. I don't see anything. I walk towards the closet and look in. I notice nothing out of the ordinary, pull out a robe, and close the door. While wrapping up my naked body, I reason with myself that perhaps I was just tired and forgot.

Yeah, that's it, I tell myself. I still want to lie down, but instead, I pull the covers up halfway making up the bed, trying to make the room look neat. I walk out into the front room, and Lucy follows. I notice my keys sitting near my computer and instantly, I remember Joe.

"Oh my God!" I say aloud, running to the door, opening it. *How did I get home? Is my car here?* I see my car, in my usual parking space, right beside my neighbor

Gary's motorcycle. I blink, closing my eyelids tightly for a few seconds, and then allowing them to open into a stare. The car was indeed there. Dirty, but nonetheless, there. *I don't remember driving home. I don't remember getting my keys. I don't remember Joe letting me in. I don't remember leaving the library.* I shake my head in disbelief, thinking I must be getting old and step back into the apartment, shutting the door behind me.

Suddenly the sounds of scratches and whimpers invade my eardrums, causing an instant annoyance to my already aching head. I realized Lucy is the culprit. *Ooops!*

Cracking the door open wide enough to let her inside, I say, "I'm sorry girl." If I didn't know better, I think she rolled her puppy dog eyes at me. "Naaaaa," I say aloud, while watching her scamper off to get a drink of water. I try to swallow the spit that was collecting orally, but my throat feels like the Sahara. *I should have drunk some water behind those pills.*

Making my way to the kitchen sink, I turn the cold water on, cup my left hand under the stream, and bring it to my mouth making a slurping sound as I attempt to get my throat wet. Initially, more water rolls down my chin than down my throat. The process is successfully completed after several attempts. To look at me, one would think I didn't own a single cup. But, truth be told, I liked the game the water played with me. And, I played back, holding in the wetness, trying not to let one, single drop slip between the cracks of my fingers. The water reminds me of myself, wanting to continue on its intended journey, but breaking away drop by drop; trying to find a more interesting route. I bend forward against the sink and watch intensely as the water flows down the drain. I wonder, *which pipe would it be happier in?* I push the handle down, stopping the flow. *It doesn't have a choice.* Then, I wipe the moisture from my lips with the back of my right hand. *I have a choice.*

Turning my back to the sink, I lean against it, yawning. As the hot breath escapes my mouth, I resist again the desire to return to the comfort of my queen-sized bed. My tired legs allow me to head to the living room. I begin walking towards the computer, till my peripheral notices the handbag *How could I have forgotten that?*

I take a seat on the couch and let the contents of the bag spill onto the coffee table in one swoop. The tube of lipstick rolls onto the beige carpet in front of me. I bend to pick it up and hold it in my hand. I've never used this brand before, only seen it the ads of fancy magazines. Never thought it was for women of color. I tend to use the cheap Wet 'n Crazy brand you can get at the dollar stores. Surprisingly, it doesn't break my sensitive skin out.

Makeup doesn't meet my skin too often. And, if

it does, I'm just playing around at home, trying different application techniques. When I'm in the mood, I'll take pictures of myself with my computer camera and post them on my web pages. The guys seem to like them. They tell me I'm sexy and some nights I believe them. At times, I trust their comments enough to show them just how sexy I can be, by showing parts of me that shouldn't be seen. It's exciting to know someone is turned on by the sight of me. Even if it is a complete stranger. Even if it is only for that one night. Even if it is only on the internet.

I open the tube to reveal an interesting color, like mauve fought burgundy and won. Intrigued, I turn the tube over and squint, making out the words 'Nude Splurge'. Still sitting, I let the creamy shade find my lips on its own, first the bottom then the top. Immediately, I feel sexy. *Is this what Jessica feels like on a daily basis?* I hold that feeling for a moment until I feel the need to see what I look like. Rushing over to the mirror in the hallway, I almost trip. Looking down, I see nothing, decide that I need to vacuum, and continue on to my reflective destination. I look in the mirror and disappointment sets in. *Ughh.* Feeling sexy and being sexy are indeed two different things. But I kiss my reflection anyway, leaving a perfect round lip print.

Wishing I had someone to really kiss, I return to the sofa, laying back on the cushions. Placing the closed lipstick tube down, I think of Marvin, my ex-fiancé. He was so attentive. He brought me flowers and took me out to nice restaurants. He held the door open for me like a gentleman. He even walked on the outside of the sidewalks to protect me from traffic. We could talk about anything, from the latest television show to the war in Iraq. I thought he was perfect.

That is, until the day I came home to find him on my sofa with his pants around his ankles and his penis in my best friend's mouth.

Lareesa Fonville Willis

Chapter 10
Shame On You

Vonya was a whore from back in the day. I should've known better than to let her around my man. She was only my best friend because I didn't have many friends to choose from in school and our mamas were friends.

She also stood up for me in school when kids would pick on me for one reason or another. Most of the time, they teased me because of my weight.

After the Manny nightmare, my young mind decided that I didn't want to be pretty anymore. Since the television said that fat girls were ugly. I decided that I was going to be fat. I started eating everything in sight. I would hide food in my room. Every spare nickel I got, I spent on Twinkies, chips, or any other fattening foods. I wouldn't participate in gym activities and I never played outdoors.

The kids would call me names. One that stuck was 'Cynthia the blimpia'. They would say it over and over while filling their cheeks with air and waddling around me like penguins. I would try to act like it didn't bother me, but it did. *I wonder how many other kids got fat on purpose.* I learned how to stop crying in front of them, but I most definitely cried when I got home. I would look at myself in the mirror till my tears made the image go away. Then I'd lie on my bedroom floor with my eyes shut tight imagining I was in a different place, a different time.

Early on, I imagined getting on a space ship and traveling to a planet where nobody knew me or my past hurts. The place would be full of marshmallows and no men were allowed to enter. No bad mamas were there either.

As the years went by, my imagination developed, just like my body. I'd picture myself thin and grown on a tropical island somewhere so perfect it didn't exist. I'd imagine a black string bikini around my petite frame and wavy hair flowing down my back, all natural of course. My dreams never involved the weaves my reality consisted of. I imagined a tall, muscular fellow wanting every inch of my body. I saw a model in a car advertisement once that literally became the man of my dreams. I named him Pedro and he gave my pre-teenage thoughts something to really think about.

One day, while thinking of my paper boyfriend, without realizing it, my hand wandered to my crotch. I felt a sensation I'd never known before. I felt dirty and pulled my hand away. A sermon that Grandpa Manias' pastor, Bishop Cornelius Ricer, preached one Sunday came rushing back to me. The preacher said that it was wrong for people to touch themselves sexually. He said we would be damned to hell for eternity for doing so. I didn't know much about hell at the time. I just knew it was hot and if you didn't accept Jesus Christ as your savior you'd go there after you died. Well, Grandpa Manias had already convinced me to ask Jesus to come into my heart so I thought I had nothing to worry about. Bishop Ricer said that hell was where bad people went to be punished. He showed the congregation a disturbing movie that I don't think any child should be susceptible to. It showed a dark, hot, gruesome place with an unquenchable fire. There was no water in sight and the people were begging for relief from the torment. They were crying but I saw no tears. They were grinding their teeth to bits because of the pain. Cries for forgiveness were spoken, but it was too late. We saw insects eating people's flesh, crawling into their open wounds. The groans and moans were unbearable to listen to. It was beyond what you'd see in any horror flick these days. Freddie Kruger ain't got nothin' on Satan. It caused me nightmares for years. *I didn't want to go to hell, no sir. I surely did not.*

I had also heard from some kids at school that you could go blind if you touched your own privates. I didn't want to go blind, either. But, the wandering hand syndrome I was developing seemed to happen more often than not. Whenever I realized I was touching myself, I quickly stopped and did something else.

One day after school, I threw caution to the wind and decided to forget. I forgot about guilt. I forgot about going blind. And, I forgot about going to hell. *I wanted my twelve-year-old body to feel good.* Although I was home alone, I locked my bedroom door, took off all my clothes, and allowed my hands to explore my body. I touched my breasts and nothing in particular happened. Then, I laid down and spread my legs a little, giving my fingers permission to explore. I rubbed the short, curly hair gently until my privates started to tingle. I didn't know it then, but I was aroused. It felt so good and I didn't want the feeling to stop. I continued rubbing until a weird sensation came over my body. It was strange, but good and I continued the ride, curious as to how it ends. I felt a couple a muscles contract and then I started to hurt. *Uh, oh!* I got scared and laid there, very still, waiting to see if I was going to go blind. I blinked a few times and the feeling subsided. *Whew!* I looked around my room. I could still see my black and white television. I could still see my Nintendo. I could still see my cabbage patch doll, Rachel. I could still see my Smurf clock. *Oh, my God! Look at the time! Mama will be home soon.* I quickly repented, got dressed, unlocked my door, and took the homework out of my book bag, making it like just another ordinary day at the Evans' household.

After that day, I rushed home nearly every day to be myself, with myself. Most of my childhood is a blur because I spent most afternoons wrapped up in the arms of my lover, myself. This continued for years, through high school and then college. I was beginning to think I had a serious problem. While other girls had boyfriends, I had vibrators. I think that's why when I met Marvin, I clung to him. I could get out of this self-gratification and repent ritual that I did. Here was someone who actually wanted me and I obliged without hesitation. We met right after I was promoted from intern to librarian at the library. He was doing a research paper on the American Justice System and didn't have a clue where to begin. He was cute and one of the first guys to show a real interest me. I pretty much wrote his paper for him. To thank me, he took me out to Darryl's restaurant on Midlothian Turnpike. I had the chicken fingers, he had a colossal club. He told me over dinner that I was special and that he wanted to be in my life forever. You know what? I believed him.

A few months later, we went back to that same restaurant, where he surprised me by popping the question.

Marvin and I haven't been together in 1 year, 4 months, 2 days and...11 hours, 33 minutes, I think as I glance at the nearby clock. *Yep, I still remember* the exact time I caught them. Mainly because when I walked in on them, he gave me some bogus excuse of how he was timing her on how long it would take him to cum. He tried to tell me about some stupid bet they made while his penis was in her mouth! They never stopped, paused, nothing. Her head was bouncing up and down in his lap while she waved at me standing at the front door! I was literally in shock. The only thing I felt other than my heart breaking was the hot tears flowing down my cheeks. I couldn't move. I wanted to go choke him, then her. No, her, then him. I didn't care which one lost the ability to breathe first. I wanted them removed from my sight, from my apartment, from my world. I'd never felt hate before, but I imagined this must be it. My tears turned from fiery hot to ice cold, almost frozen. Time seemed to do the same.

I didn't remember walking to my bathroom, but I'm sure that's how I got there. I spent the entire night on the cold tile floor, crying. At least, that's what my tear stained face, blood shot eyes, and trembling body told me. I didn't hear them finish. I didn't hear them leave. It took Lucy whimpering and scratching at the door for me to even move. It hurt for me to look around. I felt many different things. Weak. Used. Worthless. Violated. This was the man I was going to spend the rest of my life with. I gave my heart to him and he crushed it like it was nothing. I thought I knew him. And, he did it with her of all people. *Why did it have to be with her?*

If I had to relive that devastating moment all again, I almost definitely would've made a detour for my knife drawer in the kitchen. Something else would have been scarred that night, other than my heart. I should have done a Lorena Bobbitt on his cheating tail. I should have acted like I was going to join in and snip, snip! He, nor his small member, would've been worth pulling jail time, though. I keep telling myself that everything happens for a reason. I just wish somebody would tell me what the reason is.

I spent the next day eating everything I could find in my apartment. I vomited at least three times and continued to force feed myself. I needed something else to hurt on me other than my heart. I wanted to crawl up in a knot and die. If it weren't for Lucy, I probably would have. She wouldn't leave my side the whole time. It's funny how a dog can make you feel better in the worst situations.

Vonya was a whore and I knew she was a whore. *Why on God's green earth did I let her around my man? I shouldn't have let her around him!* I've seen her sleep with anyone just for kicks. In fact, that's how she got through college.

She had the name Superhead long before that Ms. Hollywood Video chick did. She has no morals. But, it's not her fault. Her mother never cared about what she did. Her mama put her on birth control at eleven years old. She allowed Vonya to have boys in her room. They were even allowed to spend the night. She worked late hours at the hospital and was rarely at home to parent Vonya. She's had three abortions and two sexually transmitted diseases. If I didn't know better, I'd think she was trying to beat the world sex record or something. I don't know what she was trying to prove by being with all these men. I really hated to be associated with her because some of the boys thought I put out like she did. I didn't want that kind of reputation. But, I had to be around them because my mother loved Vonya and her mother, Ms. Tonya. *Ughh.*

I disliked the fact that their names rhymed. The sperm donor's name was Vincent. Hence, the V. He comes around every so often when he wants something, like a place to crash for a few nights. He's strung out, but Ms. Tonya loves him. She keeps trying to put him in different rehab programs, but he keeps leaving. You can't help a crackhead that doesn't want to be helped.

Vonya has never had a real relationship with her father. She told me one time that he tried to sleep with her. She said he thought she was her mother. Then all of a sudden, she was pregnant by him and had to get rid of the baby. There's a big difference between trying to have sex and actually having sex. The story had so many holes in it that I referred to it as the Swiss lie for a while; inside my own head, of course. I wouldn't dare tell a soul, especially since it didn't seem like I had the whole story and I didn't want to stir up any trouble. Vonya eventually told me what really happened one day while we were playing truth or dare. I think she wanted to finally get it all out, because she usually always picked dare. All I asked was, "Do you love your father?" and she responded with a yes that was unapologetic. She went on to tell me how their sexual relationship started. She said one night he came into her room while she was sleeping and got in bed with her. She said she woke up with him on top of her, already inside her, pumping the little innocence she had left away. She told me how she didn't try to get him to stop. She said it made her feel like a real woman that he chose her over her mother. I wanted to remind her that he was strung out on drugs and his choices weren't very sound, but I refrained. She said she started pretending that she was asleep, even if she were awake so he would still come in and be with her. One time, she had made the mistake of waiting up for him. He cussed her out, called her a slut, and slapped her across the face. He didn't want it given to him, he wanted the control. He wasn't in control of his life and he needed to be in control of her, at least in that way. He needed that power and he had to take it, while she was sleeping. The only time he told her he loved her was when he was molesting her. A sad reality, but she accepted the way he showed his love, and she loved him in return.

Vonya has called me several times since the betrayal, the last time being a couple months back. I just let the machine pick it up and never return her calls. I don't have anything to say to her, ever.

After remembering all that, I sigh. I rub my lips together, allowing the silkiness of the lipstick to have its way with the creases of my mouth. I still want to be kissed. I haven't seen Marvin since he cheated on me. I hate to say it, but I miss him and still long for his touch. It's been so long.

"I'm pathetic," I say aloud and as if on cue, Lucy comes and sits down at my right foot.

Chapter 11
You've Got Mail

DING DONG! My eyes open, aware of my surroundings. *Oh no! I lost it! My dream*! I try to shut out the ringing and return to my nap and the man in my dreams. I close my eyes and demand Mr. Sandman to give it back.

DING DONG! DING DONG! "This better be good," I say aloud, getting off the couch and making my way to the door. I peep through the peephole to see a young, white male wearing a black baseball cap. It looks like he's holding something, but I can't tell what it is.

"Who is it?" I yell groggily through the door.

"Pizza," a male responds.

"I didn't order any pizza," I say disturbed.

"This is the address on my ticket. A large supreme and breadsticks," he says.

That's my usual order. Did I order this pizza? No! I was asleep. "I didn't order any pizza," I say again.

"Last name Evans?" he asks.

What? How did he know my last name? I know I didn't order this pizza. I was sleep. This has got to be some sort of joke. I put the chain on the door and open it enough to fully view the man. He looked innocent enough, wearing black jeans, white tee, black jacket, and baseball cap. The pizza was in a silver warmer bag.

"Listen, I don't know who ordered this pizza, but it wasn't me. I'm sorry you had to drive all the way here for nothing, but I didn't order this." I say.

The guy looks confused and started to speak, "Bu..." I close the door mid syllable and yawn, leaning my back against the door.

After his footsteps fade, I turn around and walk towards the computer. It's been a few days since I've stroked the keys. *I'm sure they missed me*, I think as I power it on and take a seat. It doesn't take long for Windows to welcome me home and I smile once all my icons greet me. I use my new mouse with the buttons on the side and connect to the internet. I log into my instant messenger and wait to the see how many of my friends are online.

Over the past year, I've made several online friends. I'm even the moderator of a Plus Sized Beauties room. The men online love big, beautiful women. It's a shame more don't in the real world. It's like they want a skinny woman on their arm, but they want a fat woman in their fantasies. I guess it's true what they say, 'more cushion for the pushin'. Seems to me the only advantage to making love to a skinny chick is you can pick her up and place her in compromising positions. But, you couldn't even get rough with her. I'm not talking go to jail rough. I'm talking 'bout putting your back into it rough. Big girls can handle it!

My friends list appears and I have 19 offline messages. *Awww, I was missed.* Six of them are from the same person, Damio. His screen name is watchouthernowww_36. Never asked him what I should be watching out for. I've known him for about eight months now and we talk practically everyday. We chat, but he doesn't have a cam so I don't know what he looks like. He's seen me on cam several times and he often tells me how beautiful I am. He claims he loves me. And, I've got to admit, I have a few feelings for him too. How can you not have feelings for someone you talk to nearly every day? He's such a sweet, honest guy. I can talk to him about anything. We'll never meet though. He lives in Italy.

I respond to the offline messages and make myself visible, hoping to bump into Jayman7819. He's 34, from Chicago, and has arms so muscular I want to reach through the computer screen every time his picture pops up. It ought to be a crime to be that fine. The night we met, we talked till the sun came up and discovered that we had a lot in common. From the way we want to raise our kids to personal goals to our favorite drink. It was almost spooky the way we connected. We've been talking longer than Damio and I have, but Jay distances himself from me. It's almost as if he is scared of his true feelings for me. See, we'll have an amazing conversation and then I won't hear from him for a while. You would think the connection would have to start all over again, but it never matters how long he stays away. We pick right back up at the same spot we left off at. Sometimes, I think he just thinks I'm some lonely, desperate broad who'll always be online for him to converse with. But, I'm not. I think I just may be in love with this cyber man. If only he would love me back, and stop being scared to take a chance on love. I'm tired of playing these games. One day we'll talk, the next day we won't. I'm starting to think he is living another life. But, how is that possible? Sometimes we talk to the wee hours of the morn. And sometimes, it's on cam. I don't see anyone else around. He even gave me a tour of his condo. It didn't have much in it. Typical man décor: Big flat-screen TV, leather furniture, no wall art, ironing board up in the living room, bottles of Gatorade or water could be seen all over. Nothing special, but I could imagine coming home to it on a regular basis. He talked about sending me a plane ticket one time, but it never happened. A box pops up on the screen. It's Damio.

"Bella! How my beautiful American black princess doing 2day?"

"I'm doing wonderful Damio, how are you doing?"

"Much better now. Was worried about you. Where have you been?"

"I'm sorry. These past couple of days have been really strange."

"Oh. How so beautiful?"

I want tell him everything that happened over the last few days with the purse, the feeling that I was being watched, Jessica, the late unknown visitor at my door, the security guard, the closet, and even the unordered pizza, but I didn't. I turned my head to view the contents of the handbag all over the coffee table.

I'm a thief, I thought. I'd never stolen anything before in my life. Well, there was that one time I was at the Mini Mart on Broad Rock Road. Mother and I went to the laundry mat next door to wash our sheets and comforters. I couldn't have been more than seven or eight years old. I asked her for some change to get some Now and Laters candy and she told me no, that they would rot my teeth out. I loved me some Now and Laters, especially the sour apple flavored ones. She gave me two dollars and asked me to get her some bbq pork skins and a coke. I went on and did what I was told, but as I went down the aisle to get the skins I noticed the candy. It was only five cents for four pieces! I picked up the green pack and smelled its apple goodness. I don't know what came over me. I had to taste its sour sweetness. I looked around the convenience store. Nobody was looking at me. I shoved the candy into the right pocket of my jeans in one quick motion and continued on to get the fried pork. Up at the register, I just knew sirens would sound and the police would

come out from the back to frisk me. They didn't. I paid

for the items and took them to mama. She was over

near the folding table talking to some man with a gold

tooth and pants so tight they showed his frontal bulge.

I handed her the snacks and change. Without really

looking at me, she gave me the change back and told

me to go get the Now and Laters. "But, mama, you

said...," I tried to remind her.

"Go on now, Cyn, can't you see I'm talking?"

She shooed me away as if I were a pestering insect. I

went back into the connecting store, straight for the

register. I pulled out the square green candy and placed

it on the counter. "I would like to pay for this please" I

told the lady behind the counter. "She looked at me real

funny and said, "Five cents, no tax." I gave her ten

cents and waited to receive my change. As she handed

me five pennies, she said "It feels good, doesn't it?"

"Excuse me?" my young mouth uttered.

"To pay for what you want. It feels good to be able to do it, doesn't it?"

"Yes, ma'am," I say.

She gave me an approving head nod and I left the store feeling like I'd made the right decision.

Shaking my head, I return my attention back to the conversation with Damio on the computer screen.

"I don't know. I'm just not myself" I type back.

"You want me to call you?"

"No, it's too expensive."

"I don't care. I have some time on my calling

card."

"It's ok, really it is. I have to go. I'll talk to you later."

"If that's what you want. I'll be here if you need me, ok?"

"Ok, thanks hon."

I become invisible on the messenger, get up from the pc, and plop back down on the couch.

I can't seem to remember much about last night. Maybe it was all a dream. Maybe it'll become clear on Monday when I go back to work.

DING DONG! I think, *my **God, what's with this door?*** I get up to answer it. I look through the peephole and can't believe my eyes. It's Joe!

113

Why is he here? What does he want?

"Who is it?" I say, knowing full well who it is.

"It's uh, Joe from work." He says sounding completely different from last night.

"What are you doing here?" I ask through the door.

"I want to talk to you. Can we talk?" He asks.

"About what?" I ask back.

"Can you open the door please? So we can talk." he says.

"If I remember correctly, you didn't want to open a door for me. Looks like the tables have turned,

Joe," I state.

"You have it all wrong," he tries to explain.

"Oh, I do, do I?" I question him.

"Yes, you do. I really want to just talk to you. Did the pizza come already? I was trying to get here before they brought it."

"Youuuuuu ordered the pizza? Why?" I ask, still through the door.

"Just trying to be friendly. It's the same kind you order at work," he says.

I thought about the last time I'd ordered pizza at work. "That was months ago, Joe," I say.

"I have a good memory when it comes to you," he admits.

What is he saying? I get quiet.

"Ms. Evans, I umm really like you," Joe says to the door.

He's kidding, right? Surely, he is..

"What do you mean, you really like me?" I ask.

"I mean, I've had my eye on you and I like what I see. I know you don't have a boyfriend. So, I figured why not me?"

"How do you know I don't have a boyfriend?" I ask.

"I know more about you than you think I do,"

he says.

"Joe, we don't even work together that much.
How could you possibly know about me?" I ask.

"You talk to me all the time," he states.

This man has lost his mind. "What? No we don't,"
I insist.

"Yes, we do," he claims.

"The first time we've ever really talked was
when I asked you to unlock the door to the library," I
say trying to make him understand.

He asks, "Will you please let me in so we can
talk? Should I go get a chair from my apartment?"

"Your apartment?!" *Please don't tell me you live*

117

here..

"Yeah, I live on the other side of the building. Now, will you please let me in?" he asks again.

"I'm not letting you in nowhere! Now tell me what you are talking about. What do you mean we talk all the time? I'm tired of these games!" I run to get my cordless phone just in case I need to call 911. I am back in an instant, just in time to hear…

"You may not like what I'm about to say, but I'm Damio."

What did he just say? I almost pass out. *He can't be. Impossible!* My mind begins to go over the conversations with Damio in my head.

"That's not possible," I respond.

"It's the truth," he says calmly.

"How is that possible?" I say, becoming upset.

Oh, my God! I start to think about all the lies I'd told him online. Everything wasn't a lie, but I embellished my life quite a bit. So, if I did, it is possible that he could have too.

"I'm sorry I didn't tell you before," he says.

"Go away. Leave me alone," I say, embarrassed by my life. Then, I remember that I'm talking to a security guard and not the Italian stallion I thought Damio was.

"Please, just listen," he begs. "Then I'll go away."

"I wanted to tell you so bad. Really, I did. I

wanted to tell you last night, but you passed out. I wasn't trying to play with your head. It's just that online, I can be anyone I want to be and escape reality. Isn't that what you've been doing? I don't hold it against you for wanting your life to be more interesting than it really is."

I passed out? Is that why I have this bruise on my head?

"I passed out?" I ask him.

"Yes, you did. That's the main reason I came over. I wanted to check on you because you hit your head when you hit the concrete. When I put you to bed, I noticed a bruise. I stayed with you for a while to make sure you were ok."

"What?! You put me to bed? Did you drive me home, too? My God! This is too much! How did you know where I lived?"

"You told me that," he says.

"I thought you said I was passed out. See, you are lying. I knew it," I accuse.

"I'm not lying. You told me online," he says.

Oh no!! He's right! I did! How could I have been so stupid? I thought he lived in Italy! I say nothing for a moment trying to put all this together.

"Damio or Joe or whoever you are, please leave before I call the police." I warn, meaning every word.

I walk away from the door leaving him on the other side and back to the sofa I go. *I can't process this information right now. I just can't.*

Lareesa Fonville Willis

Chapter 12
Answering the Call

Jessica's cell phone rings and knowing I shouldn't, I answer it anyway. Flipping the phone up, I listen to the breathing on the other end, scared to say hello.

"Uh, hello, Jessica?" A man's voice asks.

I want to hang up but I can't. I cough and manage to answer with the word, "Yes?"

"Hi, a friend of mine gave me your number. I have something you'll be interested in. Meet me at the Holiday Inn Courtyard, Rm. 134 at 10 tonight. You won't regret it."

The voice sounded rushed, like he had to hurry and say it or he would lose the nerve. He pauses as if awaiting a response. I don't oblige him with one and I wondered if he could hear my heart beating through the phone.

"I look forward to meeting you tonight babe." He hangs up as if the meeting was confirmed.

What is this woman into? Something she'll be interested in? I shrug off the phone call and grab the television remote control. I need to escape my reality. *Maybe I can get lost in a good movie and forget about everything.* Flipping through the channels, I see the same old thing: happy people, living exciting lives.

It's Saturday and I'm sitting at home, alone again. This time, it's by choice, but it's still depressing. My thoughts turn to Damio. *Was he serious? No, ewww, was I serious for even talking to him?* I shake my head in disgust. *He sent me a fake picture. Wait, did he? No, that's right I started talking to him without seeing a picture of him. He never showed me a picture! And, I never asked him for one. What a stupid mistake!!! We just hit it off so fast that I never thought about it. I mean, looks don't matter that much but, Italy? Seriously? He lives in the same apartment complex? Really? Why didn't he just tell me the truth? I can't believe the whole friendship was a lie. Why am I so stupid? And, I still don't know what happened the other night. He was in my apartment! I need to get out of here. Maybe I should go meet the man that called. Yea, I should. He doesn't know what she looks like. He's just a friend of a friend. But, could I pull it off? Has he seen a picture of her? We kind of have the same facial features. Maybe he'll think she just got fat. I could even wear her perfume and the makeup she had in the purse.* Thoughts go back and forth in my head.

"Naaaaa," I say aloud, trying to put the thought out of my mind. I hear a buzzing sound coming from the computer. It's some guy who saw my profile, wondering if we can cam tonight. *Uggggh! This is not going to be my existence anymore! It's time I made an appearance in the real world.* That message made me decide to definitely go. *Yea, I'm not 'gonna be Cyn tonight.*

Chapter 13
Secret Rendezvous

Ten o' clock sharp, I arrive at the Holiday Inn Courtyard, looking sexier than I've ever been. I really didn't know what to wear. I decide on a black dress I'd bought right before Marvin and I split. It is a little tight, now that I've gained weight, but in all the right places. I knock on the door to room 134 and get no answer. I look around and notice a couple going into a nearby room, giggling. Another view, I see a man staring me down and I knock again, this time harder. The door opens and the room is pitch black. I want to turn around and run, but I'm here now. I hear a voice says, "Come on in, I won't bite." I take a deep breath and cross the threshold. The door closes behind me in a thud. My eyes adjust to the darkness and I see the

127

image of a man. I can't make out his face, but I can tell he is well built and tall.

"Have a seat sweetheart," he says as he leads me by the hand to the king-sized bed. His voice was so smooth it rolled from my ears to my soul. I was no longer afraid. He couldn't see me and I couldn't see him, but there was calmness in the air. I sat down on the edge of the bed and the stranger took his place beside me. I trembled slightly only because it had been so long since a man was that close to me. It felt good. He smelt good, like cedar, mint, and musk, all hitting your senses individually. One behind the other, intoxicating me. He came in closer as if he were smelling me. He was. I could feel the air from his nostrils on my neck. I felt like a woman at that moment. Sexy, beautiful. I leaned into him, making him kiss the spot he was near. He took advantage of the offer, by kissing me ever so gently. I didn't know kisses could be that soft. It made my body tingle and I leaned my head back, giving him a permanent invitation. He

RSVP'd by giving his lips and then his tongue a formal

introduction to my body. He then touched my face with

his right hand turning it to him. I knew he was about to

kiss me. He paused and inhaled, getting high off the

aroma coming from my flesh. After he exhaled, his

mouth found mine, planting a sensual kiss. I let out a

moan, surprising myself. I felt that kiss everywhere,

including my toes. He kept pausing and seems to be

content with just being near me. I felt a small drop of

liquid fall between my bosom, a tear perhaps. I didn't

question it because I didn't want him to stop.

Please don't stop.

"You always smell so good, baby," he whispers.

Always? Did I hear him right?

I push the thought out of my head and let him

continue exploring my mouth. I was melting. If I was insecure before, you wouldn't know it now. It all disappeared the instant he kissed me. This man wanted me. And, I wanted him to want me. I made a decision then and there to let him have me.

He must've been reading my mind, because he stood up and pulled me up from the bed. Standing in front of me, he slowly undressed me, removing everything but my heels, and placed me back on the bed. It only took him seconds to remove his clothing and join me. He climbed on top of me, feeling like a warm comforter on a cold winter day. My nipples were hard as rocks and my nether region started to flow. He kissed me so passionately, like his life depended on pleasing me. His tears were confirmed when I felt liquid drops on my face as well. *Wow, it must've been a long time for him too.* He kissed every inch of my body. And I do mean, every inch. From the front to the back, from the top to the bottom. If there was a heaven on earth, this was it. My body traveled a new journey and pulsated when it discovered new destinations.

A rest stop was inevitable as he whispered, "I know you don't want children right now so I have protection," in my ear.

Wait, how did he know that?

He kissed me, breaking my thought, and got off the bed. I hear him fumble with something and in an instant; he is on top of me. My hand pierces through the darkness to feel his penis. Once I locate the latex ring near the base, I pull my hand back, allowing my mystery man to do his thing.

Gently, he finds my womanly opening and enters me. I shudder as he makes his way deep within my core. He lets out a moan and right then, my levee breaks. I hold on to him for dear life as my walls contract around his member. *Whoa, he made me cum with one stroke! It has been a long time.* The milking sensation must have been too much for him, because a few seconds later he tenses up and I feel warmness shoot into the condom. He kisses me, collapses to my left and starts to stroke my hair. Nobody's ever stroked my hair before. It made me feel loved. I could imagine how this made Jessica feel. Having different men express their feelings differently. I didn't need lots of men, I only needed one. A sole partner to share everything with. My home, my body, my mind, my life, everything. Yea, I only needed one.

I am so relaxed. I want to stay here in this stranger's arms forever. I don't want to move, but my bladder is full. It never did do what I wanted it to. I was fourteen before I stopped wetting the bed regularly. So, you can imagine how many slumber parties I went to. You guessed it, none. I longed to be a normal child with dry sheets. I imagined life would've so much happier without a rash on your stomach and thighs. I grew up thinking it was normal for soap to burn your body. My breathing starts to get heavier. The last thing I need is to fall asleep in this hotel and wake up in a puddle. And even more than embarrassment, they say you can get a bladder infection if don't urinate after sex. I surely didn't need that.

I stay there for a few moments longer till his hand stops moving and I think he's asleep. I crawl out of bed and slowly head for the bathroom, trying to be careful not to trip in the dark. I bump into a desk chair noisily, proving my attempt futile. *Ouch!*

"Do you need the light on sweetheart?" he asks, startling me. "I don't want any bruises on you baby."

"Oh," I giggle, "I thought you were asleep."

"No, just resting my eyes. Loving you took alot

out of me," he said turning over. Let me get my baby some light." he says while reaching for the lamp beside the bed. In two clicks, light filled the room, while shock and confusion filled his face.

"You are not my wife!" he exclaims. The light blinds me and I blink a couple of times trying to focus my eyes.

"What?" I say, naked and confused.

He panics, "You are not my wife. Where is Jessica, my wife? Oh God, I thought you were my wife!!"

"Wife?" My eyes suddenly focus. "Oh, my God. You're the man from the picture!" I say running for the bathroom to now hide my nakedness.

"Picture? What picture?" he questions me,

jumping out of bed.

I lock the bathroom door and stand behind it, thinking what a fine mess I'd gotten myself into.

"Who are you?" What is your name? And what have you done with Jessica? I swear, if you hurt her, I'll...." he stopped himself before threatening me through the door.

Oh my God. What do I say? What do I do? Wishing there was a way to escape, I look around the room. Nothing here but a shower and a toilet. For a second, I wonder if I can flush my way to freedom. *Why me?!*

Turning towards the door I say, "My name is Cyn and I didn't do anything to your wi-."

"How do I know that?" he interrupted.

"I didn't even know Jessica was your wife until you just told me a few seconds ago."

"Do you expect me to believe that?"

"It's the truth," I say sighing, hoping to be believed.

"How do you know my wife? How did you know to meet me here?"

"I...umm....don't exactly know your wife," I say.

"What do you mean, you don't know my wife?" He sounded more agitated.

"Well, she came to my job a few times, that's all."

"Where do you work?" he asks.

"The downtown library," I reply.

"The downtown library," he repeats with his words becoming distant. I knew he was walking away.

"Come out here," he demands. "I think I know who you are."

Is this some sort of trick to get me out of the bathroom? "What do you mean you know who I am?"

"I need to look at you. Come out of the bathroom," he says.

I really didn't have a choice. I can't stay in here forever. *I'm naked, in a bathroom, and I just slept with somebody's husband. I'm going to hell.* "Can you pass me my clothes please?" I ask.

He picks up my clothing from off the carpeting floor and hands them to me through the opening in the door. I make sure to brace my foot behind it just in case he decides to barge in. He doesn't.

I dress and begin to head out the bathroom when my bladder reminds me of my intended purpose. I take a moment to squat over the toilet seat and relieve my full organ. *Whoa, that felt good.* I flush and open the door to wash my hands at the basin inside the room. *Why do they make hotel rooms like this? Sinks should be in the bathroom.* I wash my hands as slow as possible to prolong the conversation that awaits me. I notice him in the mirror, sitting on the bed, half dressed, eyeing me, trying to calmly collect his thoughts. I try to make small talk to lighten things up.

"You know, this soap is so drying to the skin." *I couldn't come up with anything better than that?*

He doesn't respond.

"It really is. That is probably why they put the little bottles of lotion in here." *I sound stupid.*

He still doesn't respond. I decide to zip my mouth and dry my hands on the white hand towel hanging on the shelf.

Turning around, I lean against the basin, not wanting to sit near him on the bed.

"Your last name is Evans, right?" he asks.

I look at him in disbelief. *How is it that all these people know me all of a sudden? What's really going on?*

"It's Evans, right?" he asks again, knowing full well that the answer was already on my face.

"Yes," I say, not wanting to confirm it for obvious reasons. "How do you know me?"

"I don't know you. I know of you," he responds.

"Excuse me?" Confusion is apparent and I want answers.

"You've been the talk of my house for the past year," he confesses.

"What are you saying?" I ask, moving over to the bed.

"Look at you. Same hair texture, yours is shorter, but the same. Same facial features. You have to look real hard, but its there. Same height.... "

"What are you saying?" I repeat, cutting him off.

"Same color eyes, too. She wears contacts, though." He continues.

"What?" I utter.

"You even smell like her. But, how can you? That's her unique scent. We made it together at a perfume factory in the Bahamas. It's not on the market. You couldn't have purchased it anywhere."

He stands up getting worried again. "What did you do to her? Oh, God. What did you do?"

"I told you, I didn't do anything to her," I say.

"I called her cell phone. Even when she doesn't come home, she answers her phone," he claims.

"She lost her phone," I state.

"She lost it? Then why hasn't it been reported lost? I spoke to her earlier today. We made arrangements to meet."

"That was me on the phone," I admit.

He questions, "That, was you?"

"Yes," I answer. "She left her purse at my job and I took it. You happy now?"

"I don't understand. How did you end up here?" He walks over to the table near the door, but he doesn't bother to sit.

I sigh and tell him how I wanted to live on the edge for once in my life.

"Do you know how this could've ended up? This is insane! You can't go around meeting complete strangers at night in hotel rooms!" He scolds me.

"Tell your wife that." I didn't mean for it to come out like that, but it did.

He looks like it is taking everything in him to not to slap me. He just stares up at the ceiling like he can see through it, straight up to heaven. "I've tried to. She won't listen to me," he says.

I don't know what to say, so I wait for him to speak.

"Our relationship has been messed up lately. A lot of things have been going bad for us the past couple of years. She won't listen to anything I have to say. I was hoping tonight would change something for us. I was hoping she would see that I could be spontaneous and love her the way she needed to be loved. I pray for her constantly. Running around with this guy or that guy. But you know the real danger? The real danger is in loving somebody too much. It's sad when you know it's their heart you can't trust."

He comes back over to the bed and sits down, looking emotionally drained.

"If you have her phone, I can't even get in touch with my own wife," he thinks aloud. Turning towards me, he asks, "Do you know how to get in touch with her?"

"No. Wait, yes, she gave me a phone number on a card," I remember.

"Where is the card?" he asks.

"I don't know, I hadn't planned on calling her,"
I say.

"Call your sister and find out where she is," he
says.

What did he just say? "Excuse me?" I question
him.

"Find out where she is," he repeats.

"You said, my sister," I say, in disbelief.

"Yes, my wife Jessica is your twin sister," he
says like should've already known.

This can't be true. "Did I miss something here?"

"Haven't you been listening to anything I've

been saying? Geesh, and she said you were the smart one."

I try to process the information that was just presented to me. *I have a sister. I have a twin sister. And its Jessica? No freakin way.*

I watch as he puts the rest of his clothes on just as fast as he took them off hours earlier.

As if it just dawned on him, he says, "I broke my vows tonight. No matter what she's done, I vowed to remain faithful and I've just cheated on my wife."

He starts pacing the floor back and forth, mumbling or praying, I couldn't tell which.

"You haven't cheated. You didn't know. This can be our little secret."

"No, it can't. God knows all," he says looking defeated.

"Yea, well, since God knows all, then he knows that you thought you were making love to your wife." I pause and say, "I'm truly sorry. This is my first time doing anything like this. I just wanted to be someone totally different than who I really am. I've been so lonely lately. I just wanted to feel good. To feel special. To feel like a woman. If only for one night."

I start to feel bad and decide to put the blame back on him. "You know this wouldn't have happened if you hadn't called pretending."

He begins to get defensive, "Oh, so now this is my fault?"

"I don't know what I'm saying, ok? Look, it's nobody's fault and nobody has to know." He looks at

147

me and knows that I'm being for real.

"Ok, this stays between these walls. It goes no further than this. This would be a scandal if my congregation found out," he says.

I know he didn't just say congregation. I choke, "Congregation?"

"Yes, I'm Pastor Jimmy Persugla of Fifth Mt. Sinai Holy Church on Venable Street," he says walking over to the mirror.

Words began forming in my head, but none were bold enough to come out of my mouth. He asked me if I was I ok and all I could do was nod my head. He grabs his belongings and leaves me in the hotel room to listen to the clutter inside my head.

What have I done? I just had sex with a minister. Hot,

amazing sex with a minister. A minister who is also my twin

sister's husband? Oh yea, I'm going straight to hell.

Lareesa Fonville Willis

Chapter 14
Born Again

Exiting the hotel room, the sunlight hurt my eyes. As they adjusted to the morning sun, I feel something or someone bump into me, knocking me to the concrete floor, my head nearly missing the rail.

"Hey, watch where you're going." The voice sounds so familiar.

It takes me a moment to recognize that I'm ok and I slowly stand up. Dusting off the granules from my dress, I finally look up to the culprit. I choke on my spit and my blood begins to boil once I realize who's an arm's length away from me.

"You whore," I say, disgusted that she is in my

view. I never wanted to see this wench again, but just in case I did I had rehearsed what I would say and what fist would meet her face first.

"Look who's talking. You're the one coming out of a hotel room. I, on the other hand, work here." she said like she was proud of it. I look Vonya up and down and notice she has a maid's uniform on.

Foregoing my rehearsed speech, shake my head at her, and attempt to walk away, not wanting to waste my breath on her.

"Cyn," she tries to stop me, her tone changing. "I have something I've wanted to say to you for a very long time now. Please wait."

I stop, but only because my feet wouldn't listen to my head. I've had enough drama for one day. *What could this heffa possibly have to tell me?* I keep my back to her.

"I left you several messages. You never returned any of my calls. And I don't blame you. Really I don't." She paused. "Cyn, will you look at me? Please?"

I turn around and view the woman who'd shaken my world. Who crossed the unspoken line every friend has. I look her in the eyes.

"Cyn, I'm sorry. What I did was wrong. You were the best friend I ever had and I hurt you so much. I'm truly sorry," she says.

I wasn't ready to forgive and I could tell that she knew it.

"Just like that?" I chuckle. "I'm supposed to forgive you just like that?"

"Look, I'm not the same person I was back then. I've changed. I accepted Jesus and He washed away my sins. All of them. They are covered under the blood."

"The blood, huh?" I ask, not really asking.

"Yes, the blood. I know I did some messed up things in my life. I can't change my past, but God forgave me. He loves me despite of what I've done and I'm asking you to do the same. I've missed our friendship."

Not only can I hear her sincerity, I can see it. A tear falls from her eye and I don't know what to say. I shake my head in disbelief.

"You don't have to believe me, she says as I notice the cross she is wearing around her neck. *Maybe she is telling the truth.*

"Listen, I'm getting baptized next Sunday, at Fifth Mt. Sinai after the 11 'o clock service. I'll love it if you were there," she says.

Fifth Mt. Sinai? Did she really just say Fifth Mt. Sinai? No way in hell.

"Fifth Mt. Sinai?" I repeat to making sure I'd heard her correctly.

"Yea, the same one your gramps took us to for that vacation bible school that time. Seems like ages ago. You remember?"

My eyes squint a little, making it easier to retrieve the memory. "That's the church?" I ask, remembering. "Yea, the basement bathroom still has our names written in the stall," she says smiling. I notice then that one of her teeth is missing.

155

My mind went back. Some lady had told Grandpa Manias about the vacation bible school so he dropped us off. We couldn't have been more than ten years old at the time. Vonya didn't want to go, but I did because I wanted Grandpa Manias to be proud of me. I learned the books of the bible and some children's church songs that are still with me today. 'If You're Happy and You Know It, Clap Your Hands' and 'Deep and Wide' are a couple that come to mind. I remember one day Twinkie from the Clark Sisters showed up and played the mess out of that organ. Everybody was on their feet.

"The best friend heart is still there too," she continued, snapping me back.

"That heart was supposed to mean something," I say sarcastically.

"It did mean something. Your friendship was everything to me growing up. You were the only constant in my life, Cyn," she said, stepping in closer.

I wanted to believe her. I missed having someone around to talk to. Even though our friendship was forced, I loved Vonya. But I can't just overlook the fact that she violated my trust. "That day took something from me," I say beginning to tear up.

"I know, Cyn, I know. I was at my lowest point that day. I was high. I know that's no excuse, but all I can say is I'm sorry. Sorry for hurting the one person who let me be me. You never asked me for anything. I would like to start over and learn how to be a real friend, if you let me. Will you forgive me?"

I look up at the sky and dared the tears to fall from my eyes. Before salt water breaks me down, I turn and leave Vonya standing there, outside of Room 134.

Lareesa Fonville Willis

Chapter 15
Finding Truth

The drive home was silent, except for the voices in my head. I wish they would quiet down so I could think. *I have a sister? A twin no less. Hmph. Unbelievable!* I want to call my mother, but I decide to go see her instead. I have to hear this face to face.

I pull up to the old apartment building I grew up in. I hated that she still lived in this dump, but she says it's what she can afford.

Using my old key, I enter the apartment and a foul smell hits my nose. Collard greens are cooking on the stove and mama is sitting at the end of the dining room table working on a crossword puzzle.

"My my. Look what the cat done drug in," she says, her way of saying hello.

"Hi, mama," I say, sitting down in a chair beside her.

"You know, you don't live here anymore Cyn..."

Thank goodness! I don't respond and wait for her to continue.

"You can't just be coming on in like that," mama says.

"Do you want your key back?" I ask.

I knew she wouldn't say anything. Mama has a heart condition, sugar, gout, and a multitude of other ailments and pains. She knows she needs somebody checking on her from time to time, whether she likes it or not.

"What brings you by? And, unannounced at that?" she says not really caring, going back to her puzzle.

I cut right to the chase. "Do I have a sister?"

"So, you met her," she says, not looking up from the paper as if she knew what I was going to say.

"I've seen her," I reply.

"Jessica, come out here," Mama calls.

"What, she's here? Is she living with you?" I question, raising my voice an octave.

Mama puts the paper down. "Now calm down Cyn, she only stays here some nights when she wants to get away."

"Get awa..." Before I could finish my question, Jessica appears from down the hallway, walks into the dining room, and sits down across from me.

I don't know why I didn't see it before. I guess because I don't like what I see when I look in the mirror, but she does look like me.

"Hi Cyn," Jessica says.

So many things are going through my head. I didn't expect her to be here. "Hi," I reply back.

There is an awkward silence, but I had questions and I needed some answers.

"I feel like I'm the only one not in on the joke," I say, breaking the silence.

"This is no joke," Jessica responds.

"No, it certainly is not," Mama adds.

"Then why am I the last to know?" I add.

"I didn't know how to tell you," Mama says, almost choking on the words. I'd never witnessed her having trouble telling me something. This is different.

"You've never had a problem telling me anything before," I say bluntly.

"This is hard for her, can't you see?" Jessica asks me.

I look at my mother and remember all the hurtful things she did to me in the past. Never calling me by my full name. Treating me as if I was some burden left on her doorstep. Not protecting me from the Manny's of this world.

"This isn't hard for her. She's acting. You don't know her," I tell this look-a-like stranger. "This is hard for me! Everybody's been in on it, the little family secret."

"If it makes you feel any better, I just found out about a year ago, when my mother died," Jessica says.

"Your mother?"

"Your aunt YaYa raised me as her own," Mama says.

"Aunt YaYa, I don't have an aunt YaYa," I say, confused.

"You did," mama interrupts. "We stopped speaking right after you were born."

"Why?" I ask.

"Yolanda was always jealous of the relationship your father and I

had. She didn't know the bad, only the good. I ended up giving birth at home because we didn't have the money to pay a hospital. Yolanda was in school to be a nurse, so she helped me and your father with the delivery. At the time, I only thought I gave birth to one child and it suited me just fine having one. Truth be told, I didn't want the one. The way it had to be. It was hard on my soul, the way you was conceived and all. Anyway, I passed out from the pain. I had no idea it was two babies that done come out of me. Not till later. She took your father from me. I didn't know she would steal my child right from under me too."

Mama got up and looked out the window.

"I wanted his children, but not like that. She turned and looked at me and said, "You have always reminded me of that horrible night. The night the man I loved took not only my body, but my spirit. I never loved anyone like I loved him and I never thought he would violate me. Not ever. But he did." She sat back in the chair to finish her crossword puzzle. "You all turned out alright. No real harm done, now is it?"

No real harm done? Did she just say no real harm done? It's too much for me to take and I get up and walk outside. Jessica followed me.

"I know it's a lot to take in and we still don't have all the answers, but you gotta stay calm." I wanted to go off, but being near her calmed me.
"Do me a favor. Go home and open the envelope," she says.

"I told you, I don't hav...," she stops the lie

from leaving my lips.

"In my purse, go home and open the envelope."

Jessica repeats.

Lareesa Fonville Willis

Chapter 16
The Letter

Once home, I walk Lucy and make a turkey sandwich before getting up the nerve to open the envelope. I eat two bites, get nauseas, and throw it in the garbage. The sick feeling subsides and I go in the living room to read the letter.

Looking at the envelope, the feeling comes back and I rush to the bathroom toilet. Missing it by a few inches, I throw up on the tile floor. Feeling better, I wash my face and rinse my mouth with mouthwash, the generic minty kind.

Before I have a chance to clean my last meal off the floor, I notice Lucy chowing down. "Ewww, Lucy. That's just nasty!" I say to her.

169

After cleaning, I decide it's time to open this mysterious envelope. Inside the sealed lip, I find a handwritten letter on church letterhead.

My dearest sister,

I'm writing this letter from my bedroom floor. I spent the night here crying, wondering why my life was built on years of lies and hurt. I'll never completely understand why they did what they did....why they separated the two us.... why I thought my aunt was my mother....why I never got the chance to meet you. Now I understand why there was a hole in my heart. I've been trying to fill it with men, alcohol, and drugs, but nothing seemed to stop the hurt. It was because a piece of me was missing. Twins are not like normal people. We grew together in the womb, sharing the same space, the same food, everything. And then we were torn apart to lead totally different lives. I have a confession to make. I came to your job a few times, pretending to use the computer. I have a computer at home so I didn't need to come there. I've even followed you to your house. Once I found you, I needed to be around you. You are my missing piece, my special missing piece. Have you been feeling like something was missing from your life too? I'm the first lady at a church here on the other side of town. This is the church stationary. Sorry, I couldn't find a regular piece of paper anywhere. Anyhoo, I pretend on Wednesdays and Sundays that I'm little Mrs. Perfect. As long as I show up dressed in the latest attire, wear the biggest hat, and sit on the first row, they don't care. Not even my husband. I don't even greet the people after service anymore. An usher escorts me to the pastor's study where I sip on orange juice till it's time to go. You had a niece. Her name was Cynthia, too. Funny, I didn't know you existed when I named her. She suffocated in her crib two years ago. I guess God didn't think I would make a good mother. Sorry about the tear stains. I can't help it and I hope you can read my handwriting. I'm going to wrap this up now, but I hope you can feel me. I mean, I hope you can understand my words, even the unwritten ones. I'm sending you a message through my heart, straight to yours.

I love you.

Jess

I held the paper close to my heart so close I hoped it would penetrate through. My own tears mixed with hers, and I swear something magical took place. I couldn't put my finger on it, but indeed something happened.

I felt refreshed, like years of weight lifted off my shoulders. I had been missing something. But, I also felt pain. Like I could feel the pain she was going through. From the death of her daughter to the pain of living a constant lie.

Sitting down to check my email, I see a message from Jay telling me he'll be in Norfolk for a few days around New Years and did I want to go to some fraternity ball. Any other time, I would've jumped at the chance. But now, I didn't know if an internet romance was right for me. I closed out the message and opened my instant messenger without responding.

KNOCK! KNOCK!

Who could this be? I go to the door and look out the peephole. It's Jessica. Unlocking the door, I open it staring at my twin.

"Well, can I come in?" she asks.

"Sure," I say opening the door wider allowing her access to my domain.

"Nice place you have here," she says, looking

around.

"Thanks, have a seat," I say, pointing to the
sofa. We sit down beside each other and she notices her
belongings on the coffee table.

"So, you read the letter," she assumes.

"Yes, I did. A few minutes ago," I admit.

"I had so much more to tell you," she says.

I don't say a word.

"I still have so much to tell you," she adds.

I have a lot to tell you too, I think, wanting to come
clean about sleeping with Jim. *How can I keep this lie from
her? She would understand, especially since he really didn't know
it wasn't her. She'll just be mad at me, right?* I couldn't

convince myself so I said nothing.

"Cyn, what's wrong?" she asked, making me look her in the eye.

"Nothing. This is just all so much to take in," I say, looking away.

"I know. It is," she whispers.

"I'm sorry to hear about your daughter," I tell her. "I can only imagine what you went through."

"I'm still going through it. I relive the day I found her over and over in my head. I wasn't even gone that long. She was taking a normal nap." She began to cry and I reach out to hug her for the first time. Jessica clung to me as if her life depended on it, sobbing on my shoulder.

"It's going to be ok. Let it out. Everything is going to be ok," I say, not knowing what else to say.

She stayed there in my arms, not wanting to let me go. I wondered about all the arms she had been in and how many of them consoled her like this. I let her have all the time she needed, that is, until my arm went numb.

"Let me get you some tissue," I say breaking the embrace and getting off the couch. I return with some rolled up toilet tissue. "Sorry, this is all I have," I offer.

She reaches for it and wipes her eyes and nose. "Thank you," she says.

I sit back down beside her and we talk for hours catching up on everything we'd missed in each other's lives.

I learned that we did a lot of the same things, had the same television shows in common, spent way too much time on the internet, and had the same taste in men. She also revealed that she was bisexual, a fact that her husband wasn't willing to accept. It caused a lot of arguments and sleepless nights at the Persugla home.

I wondered about the feelings I'd felt when I saw her those times at the library. I'd never felt an attraction to a woman before. I took a chance and told her about it. She said, "We're naturally drawn to people who are similar to ourselves. You were probably just feeling the connection, our connection as twins."

I thought about what she was saying and it made sense.

A familiar buzzing sound came from my computer speakers demanding my attention.

"Excuse me," I say walking over to the computer across the room.

Noticing the box on the screen is from Damio, I send him a quick response telling him to leave me alone and I sign out of messenger.

Returning to the sofa, I start gathering Jessica's belongings and placing them inside her purse. Handing her the bag, I say, "I'm sorry I stole your stuff and I'm sorry I lied to you."

"It's ok," she says, "In fact, I want you to have it."

Her words catch me off guard and I don't know what to say, but I muster, "I can't."

"Why can't you? It means more to you than it does to me anyway. I would like to have my journal and phone back though."

"Wow. I don't know what to say," I respond and a tear threatens to spill out of my right eye.

"Thanks, would be nice," she laughs and nudges me.

"Yea, thanks. I've wanted one of these bags for a long time now."

"No problem. You should come over to the house sometime. We can see what else I have you might like."

"Are you serious?" My eyes widen.

"As a heart attack. As a preacher's wife, all I do is shop so I can look good on Sunday. Half that stuff I can't even be seen in again. I know you can't wear my clothes, but I'll accessorize you to death," she laughs.

179

I look at myself and think I'm always the ugly one. Now I'm the ugly twin.

Jessica felt like she'd said something wrong and said, "Do you know just how beautiful you are? Inside and out?"

"Huh?" I utter.

"I've been coming by the library for months. I've seen how you interact with people. It's a beautiful thing. You're so kind hearted and genuine. But, you've got to get some self-confidence."

I look at her.

"You're beautiful Cyn," she tells me.

The look in her eyes told me she was sincere. I

wanted to smile and accept the compliment, but something deep down inside made me act like I didn't hear her and I look away.

"Do you know that?" she asks. "Do I know what?" I ask back.

"That you are beautiful." I had to acknowledge the statement now. But instead of the original thankful smile, I said, "I'm not beautiful. I've never been beautiful to anyone."

"Well, my twin, you are beautiful to me. Tell me, what do you see when you look at yourself in the mirror?"

"You really want to know?" I ask.

"Yes, I really want to know," she said.

"I see a pork and bean." I said seriously.

Jessica snickers and I give her a harsh look. *I can't believe she is laughing at me!*

"I'm sorry sis, but a pork and bean? Come on", she says dragging me to a nearby mirror in the hallway. It still had that lipstick kiss on it.

"Look in it," she says.

I saw our reflections, side by side. I did look like her. I was amazed. That meant, if she's beautiful then I'm beautiful too.

I turned to my sister and smiled.

"Besides, you can't think you're but so ugly. You're around here kissing yourself in mirrors!"

We both fell out laughing.

Lareesa Fonville Willis

Chapter 17
Forgiveness

Sunday morning, I wake up uncertain of my plans. Normally my Sundays consists of Lifetime movies, the internet, and junk food all day. The past week has turned my world upside down. I wasn't in the mood for tv. I wasn't in the mood for the computer. And, surprisingly I wasn't craving anything. I turn on the radio instead and hear a soloist singing.

"Great is thy faithfulness. Great is thy faithfulness. Morning by morning, new mercies I see...."

I pause to listen to every word.

The song took me back to a simpler place and

time. I remembered hearing this song as a young girl, riding in the car with Grandpa Manias. The old Ford Nova was rusty blue and squeaked whenever you opened any of its four doors, especially the front driver's side. Grandpa had lots of 8-track tapes in that car, all gospel music. He would play them and tap his right foot while he drove. You would think the car would be jerking the way he tapped to the music, but it never did. He fancied the Mighty Clouds of Joy, a male quartet. I liked them too, although I never admitted it to him. They actually had a funky, youthful sound for it to be a group of old men singing about Jesus. Grandpa tried to teach me the ways of God. *Why didn't I listen?*

After Grandpa Manias died, I stopped going to church. I felt like God had forgotten about me, so I made myself forget about Him. I mean, I knew there was a God. There had to be someone out here greater than us all. When I was little I could feel his presence. I even had visions. Some even came true. But, I couldn't understand why God would take away the one person on this earth who truly loved me. I mean, with all the bad people in the world, why couldn't God just take one of them instead?

Grandpa Manias was a good man. He was a hardworking, family man who loved everybody. The love of his life, Ruby, passed away years before I was born. He talked about her often, sometimes even as if she were still alive. Grandpa said I reminded him of her. He even told me once that I had her quiet strength. It puzzled me when he didn't elaborate on what that meant. And I was too embarrassed to ask. I figured I'd find out someday and shrugged it off.

From what I've been told about my grandmother, she lived her life the same way she left this earth... mysteriously. They never officially determined the cause of her death from the autopsy. How does a woman die of natural causes at 28 years old? Whenever I ask mama about it, she changes the subject.

After the song, a familiar voice is heard. "Come join us this Sunday at the Fifth Mt. Sinai Holy Church, 10002 Venable Street, in historic Churchill during our 11am worship service. We will be having a special guest speaker, Pastor O. C. Davis, all the way from Brooklyn, New York. This man is anointed. We are expecting a Rhema word from God....straight from heaven...directly to the people of God. You do not want to miss this. Be in the house saints. I'll see you there." Then a woman's voice fills the airwaves "If you'd like to make a donation to Fifth Mt. Sinai, please mail them to post office box 4490120, Richmond, Virginia 23891.

Mama used to send donations to just about every televangelist on TV. It was as if she were playing the Christian lottery. She thought if she sent a dollar here or twenty dollars there, in thirty days a miracle would happen. One time, I saw her send our grocery money to some slick talking white man in red suit. He convinced her through the television that God needed her hundred dollars to help deliver her breakthrough. I don't think God got the money, because we ate beans for a month.

So, maybe that was the miracle. Even though we didn't have, we didn't go hungry. Maybe the miracle is that he still made a way. So, would we have even needed a miracle if mama had just purchased food as intended?

"Your generous donation helps us continue the Lord's work," the woman continues.

"Donation? Hmph." Why are churches always begging for money? I can see paying tithes. Grandpa Manias told me that it was mandated by God so people should do that. It's really not our money anyway. "God is just loaning it to us for a spell," he would tell me. But why do ministers get up in the pulpit and beg for people to give? They don't beg for people to stop committing adultery. He knows Elder Greg is sleeping with Sister Tameka in the mass choir, but he says nothing. He also knows Sister Monica's baby looks just like Deacon Samuel, but he keeps quiet. He doesn't beg the liars to stop being dishonest. He allowed Brother Malcolm to tell the congregation how they could make a million dollars once by joining some network marketing company. He didn't care that it was a scam. He still took his cut off the top. They don't beg the choir not to fornicate. He knows full well that the annual choir trip to Atlanta is the gospel version of Freaknic! Can we beg for some salvation and holiness instead of money?

Shouldn't it be God who reprimands saints for not giving up their ten percent? Preachers spend half of service on the subject of tithes. Shouldn't we be focusing on saving souls, not saving dollars? And, if it's not about tithing, it's about giving to the building fund or whatever fund they make up to generate some tax-free revenue.

Why do churches have building funds and never even break ground on a tree house? You gave, your children gave, and even your grandchildren gave. Now, here it is fifty years later of sowing into what you think is good ground, but nothing is springing up from that soil. Having church in a school auditorium is supposed to be temporary. If you are paying tithes every single week, sitting on metal folding chairs with a numb backside, but the pastor leaves church in an Escalade, something just isn't right.

A Kirk Franklin song grabs my attention and I start boxing the air and yelling, "This is it!" Opening the closet, I pull out a green dress and check it for wrinkles. Deciding that it'll pass, I hang it on the closet door and head for the bathroom. A quick shower later, I'm ready to slip into my church clothes. Grateful to have found a pair of hose without a run, I glide them on my legs taking extra caution. In a zip, I'm ready to go.

Walking into Fifth Mt. Sinai was strange. Vonya was right. We did come here as children. Everything looked the same, just smaller. I make my way through the vestibule into the sanctuary. The service had already started, so I take my seat beside an elderly gentleman in the rear. They are in the middle of welcoming the visitors. *Thank the Lord I missed that part.* No way did I want to have to stand up in front of everyone. I take a few seconds and scan the church for familiar faces. I notice Vonya first, sitting near the front. Then my eyes spot Pastor Persugla at the same time he seems to notice me.

We both look away, embarrassed. Jessica is there looking like a picture perfect first lady, in a purple suit with hat to match. Then, my eyes get a glimpse of something I wasn't expecting to see, my mother sitting right beside her.

The entire congregation says, "Welcome, welcome, welcome" in unison and the next part of the service begins.

The choir stands up and begins singing an off-key version of the song, 'Never Would Have Made It.' It still seems to excite the church. So much so, that one lady gets the Holy Ghost and passes out in the aisle. *I'm glad she decided to give her baby to somebody else before she got caught up in the Spirit.*

Ushers rush over to her and lay some sort of cloth on top of her. *Let me find out they give out blankets in here! I wonder if they have pillows too.*

After the choir sings, the organist plays shouting music in which everybody and their mama gets happy, including mine. This is the first time I've seen my mother dancing for the Lord. I've seen the funky chicken, the wop, and even the snake. But, a shout? Wow. *Is this for real?*

When the music stops, everyone seems to lose the spirit at once, except for one lady who still kept dancing. As far as I'm concerned, she's the only one who felt it in the first place. God doesn't automatically stop moving when the beat stops.

A man comes up to the pulpit and says, "It's offering time in the house of the Lord."

The church is silent, other than a few hand claps.

"I saidddd, it's offering time in the house of the Lord!!" he exclaims.

This time, the congregation claps and people start moving around. Women start bending over going into their purses and men reach in side and back pockets searching for dollar bills. Music starts again and gold collection plates with red velvet bottoms are passed around the room, aisle by aisle. I get out my offering and wait for a plate to visit my aisle. As I wait, I notice that the elderly gentleman sitting beside me didn't seem to have anything to offer. I place my offering inside his hand and without saying a word, I know how grateful he is. I reach back inside my purse and retrieve an additional offering. Once we gave, the choir begins singing another selection, this time in tune.

Next, the guest minister stands up to speak. *Lord have mercy. This man is fine!* I say a quick prayer that my mind stays on the sermon and not on how nice this man fills out a suit. *Amen. Help me Jesus.*

"Open your Bibles to...," I hear him say. *Oh*

shoot! I forgot my Bible. I didn't use it much, but I always kept it in a safe place. I remember the exact day Grandpa Manias gave it to me, my thirteenth birthday.

Pages start flipping all over the sanctuary. My elderly neighbor found the passage rather quickly and held the book so it was visible to me as well. I smiled.

The minister continues, "If I had to choose a title for today's message, I would title it Forgiveness." He looks up from his Bible and up to the ceiling, as if this sermon's notes were written up there.

"Forgiveness is at the heart of our relationship with God, the Father. We, precious hearts, cannot connect with God while ignoring our relationship to one other." He looks down, seemingly right at me. "I cannot love God if I don't love you." His eyes scan the room. "Y'all don't hear what I'm saying."

The congregation begins to talk back giving him satisfaction. "Uh huh's" and "Amen's" were thrown into the sermon as if on cue.

He continues, "And I can't have God's forgiveness if I don't forgive you."

I glance over at Vonya, who nodded her head in agreement, then look back at the preacher.

"We are quick to say things like, 'I can't just let her off the hook after she's-ah done me so wrong' or 'He hurt me so bad that I'm-ah never speaking to him again.'"

I adjust myself in the chair to no particular position. *This is getting personal.*

"Jesus forgave us," he added and walked to the edge of the pulpit. "And, there is no condemnation."

He clapped his hands so hard it echoed throughout the sanctuary. "Do you know what that means church?" Before we could even think about the question, he continues and says, "I mean-ah, you may have heard that all your life, but never fully understood-ah what it meant. No condemnation means..."

He begins to break down the word better than any dictionary could.

"When somebody condemns something or someone, it means that thing-ah is no longer fit for its use or its intended-ah purpose. Let's take downtown Richmond-ah for example. There are some-ah old buildings or structures if you will, that the city of Richmond-ah considers unsafe. This happens in every cit-ay. Man came up with a thing-ah called building codes. And inspectors go out and examine how fit a building is-ah for human habitation. It could be unsanitary conditions or maybe something's-ah wrong with the water." He walks to the opposite side of the pulpit and repeats himself. "I said, something-ah may be wrong with the water." He walks back to the other side, this time wiping his brow with a white handkerchief before he continues. "Maybe the electrical system is shot-ah or beams-ah are broken, threatening a collapse." He bends his large frame backwards a bit to resemble a collapse. A few people in the front stand up and wave their hands or Bible at him. "Or, it could be that the plumbing is messed up or the hole in the roof-ah has turned into a skylight. Or, a fire saints. Perhaps, a fiery blaze-ah took place. There are several reasons-ah as to why a building may be condemned." He clapped again. "I said, there are several reasons-ah as to why a building-ah is unfit to be a building. Unsafe buildings have to be repaired, it's the law. If it can't be repaired, they are-ah demolished. That's right church, they tear that sucker down!"

Can you use the word "sucker" in church? I looked

around to see if I could tell if anyone else thought the word sucker was a bit much, but the congregation didn't seem to be phased by it and were listening attentively.

Except for the few, that must have worse bladders than I do, who rush off to the restroom. *Perhaps people should wear Depends to church so they won't interrupt the*

service tip-toeing out with their pointer finger up in the air.
What's with the finger thing anyway? You're still being rude and no, you're not excused! I return my attention back to the preacher.

"Why do they tear it down church? Because it's no good to them in that-ah condition! They know-ah that if they leave it that way, it'll be a haven for crime. Drug dealers and-ah junkies and-ah prostitutes will populate-ah that building." *We can do without all the ah's on every other word Sir.*

Heads nod in agreement and a 'preach on, preacher' is heard from the audience.

"When you come to Christ, you-ah are not demolished and destroyed like that building. Oh no!" He claps again.

A plump woman in the pew in front of me says, "He's telling the truth," at no one in particular. She then proceeds to rummage through her pocketbook until she finds the butterscotch candy she was searching for and quickly puts it in her mouth.

Again, I look back at the preacher. He goes to the podium, wipes the sweat from his forehead and seemingly, looks directly at me. *Why does he keep looking at me?* I adjust myself again, this time bumping my neighbor's arm. I give a silent apology and return my eyes to the preacher.

"God doesn't put a sign on you and have you destroyed for the sins you committed in the past. You may have some structural damage. You may even have some internal damage, but God loves you and he's waiting to forgive you. It doesn't matter what you've done, he is a faithful and just God. All he needs is your permission to wipe away your damages." He looks to the other side of the room. "Ah, I'm so happy today church, to serve a God like this!"

He moves from behind the podium, walks closer to the congregation and calms his voice.

"God is not like man. Once He forgives you, it is thrown into the sea of forgetfulness. He remembers it no longer. We have a tendency of reminding God of things he's already forgotten, because we haven't gotten past them yet."

A tear falls from my eye and stuns me. I let it linger before deciding to wipe it.

"But we have to learn to let go. To keep it moving, as the young people say. Life is too short to be living a constant struggle. Worrying about something you did 20 years ago. Move on and let God heal you, completely. Be free. Don't leave here today with your same issues.

I think about all my issues. I think about all the past hurts and pains. I think about all the wrong I'd done. His words penetrate my thoughts.

"God knows what you did last night or last week. But, He still blessed you to come hear His Word. He loves you. Don't you leave here the same. No man or woman can make you feel as good as God can. You're searching for something that only exists in the true presence of the Lord. I know you can feel God tugging at your heartstrings. Let Him in." He paused

before saying, "He said, Behold, I stand at the door and

knock. Won't you answer church?"

I look around and see people wiping their eyes

and I don't feel ashamed about the tears that are falling

from mine. My neighbor passes me his handkerchief

and I nod my head as if to say 'thank you.'

"Some of y'all are up in here playing church.

Don't be a hypocrite and play with God. Some of y'all

right now are making plans in your head about who you

are going to see when you leave here today. You better

rethink that thing. God has shown me some things

about certain people in here right now. I'm not going to

call you out because He didn't tell me to do that. But

you know and I know that you need forgiveness from

the Father. Don't you know you are held to a higher

accountability based upon the position you hold?" He

pauses like God told him to stop and go another way.

"I'm talking to everyone. From myself, to the pastor to the deacon to the musicians and choir member to the ushers standing up in the back. Everyone under the sound of my voice. What's done in the dark will come to the light, sooner or later." He pauses again.

"The wages of sin is death," he says, echoing throughout the sanctuary, ringing my ears and piercing my soul. Images of that hell movie I'd seen decades ago flashed into my mind.

"Everybody who can stand, stand," he commands. Everyone rises to their feet and the choir starts to sing quietly while the preacher extends an invitation for those wanting to receive salvation.

"I want every eye closed and every head bowed. I need you to listen to what I have to say. There is nothing more important than your next decision. You can either decide to come to Christ and start life all over again. Or you can decide to stay in that pew, comfortable and in sin, and go straight to hell. I heard someone say salvation is the permission slip to enter heaven when you leave this earth. It truly is. Won't you come?"

I shift my weight back and forth from left to right, while clasping my hands behind my back.

He continues, "You may not live another day to make this decision again. You are not here by accident. You have the opportunity right now to get it right with the Master. Won't you come? Coming to Christ does not mean you are joining this church. You can go anywhere where you will be fed the truth, but I implore you today to start life anew. Give your life to the Lord."

I peep and see people flooding the aisles and clapping erupted from those I'm assuming were already saved. I start clapping too, trying to blend in.

A final, "Wont you come?" is asked by the minister and I feel as if God himself has asked me the question personally. I couldn't ignore the question. Standing here is no longer an option and I step out into the aisle to make my way to the altar. Not knowing what to expect when I got there scared me, but I continue until I reach the front of the church. I'd never been up to an altar before. Grandpa Manias asked me to repeat a salvation prayer after him while we were fishing one day on the James River. I didn't want to look around too much, but I am curious as to what is going on around me. I'm standing next to a teenage boy whose face is streaked with tear stains. *He can't be more than 14 years old.* He has on jeans, a red t-shirt, and boots. *Hmph, I could've worn jeans?* His hands are lifted high, his eyes are tightly closed, his mouth is moving, but no words are coming out. On my other side, there is an elderly lady with burgundy hair and gray roots that are in dire need of a touchup. Her hair is pulled back in a homemade bun with tiny gold beads placed throughout it. She falls to her knees and starts to clap uncontrollably. *I hope there will be someone who can help her up.* I move over a step in the opposite direction so it wouldn't be me. I glance up and notice the preacher looking straight at me. I feel uneasy because my attention was supposed to be on the Lord. He must've sensed my awkwardness and starts giving those of us at the alter instructions.

The music softens and he says, "Those of you who heeded the call of the Lord, lift your hands." Hands shoot up across the altar and he says, "The book of Romans, tenth chapter, ninth verse tells us that if we confess with our mouth and believe in our hearts that God has raised the Lord Jesus from the dead, you will be saved. When you ask Him into your heart, you are allowing Him to be the Lord of your life."

I closed my eyes and opened my heart. "I want

you to repeat after me...." he continued. In unison, we all repeated the following: "God, I recognize that I have not lived my life for you up until now. I need you in my life. I want you in my life. I acknowledge your Son Jesus Christ for giving His life for me on the cross at Calvary, and I long to receive the forgiveness you have made freely available to me through this sacrifice. Forgive me Lord. I repent. Come into my heart now, Lord. Be my Savior. Make my life anew. From this day forward, I will live for you. I will follow you all the days of my life. I ask this in Jesus' precious and holy name. Amen."

Wow. I've just made a decision to give my life to the Lord on my own! This time, it wasn't to make Grandpa Manias proud of me. This time, I didn't just say the words.

This time, I meant them. This time, I believed. With that prayer, I feel completely different. Everything that had been holding me back was now released; every weight, every struggle, every hurt, every pain. I gave it all to the Lord by giving my life to Him. Tears flowed freely from my eyes and I knew my life had just been changed forever. I wipe my wet face with the back of my hand and open my eyes. The room looks blurry and I blink to get focus of my surroundings.

"Welcome to God's family. You will never be the same," the preacher says to everyone at the altar. My insides smile and I feel pure, innocent even.

"God's family," I say to myself. *I like the sound of that.*

"Now, before you go back to your seats, I would like to come down and greet you," he says. The preacher comes down from the pulpit and shakes every new believer's hand.

I watch as he welcomes each person into God's family. When he gets to me, he pauses, looks me straight in the eyes and says, "You have been set free. Go and sin no more."

Never did I feel so free in my life! I shake my head in agreement and although my heart is light, my legs feel numb. I didn't know if my legs would carry me back to my seat. Risking the embarrassment of a possible fall, I decide to take a step. As I turn around to make the trip back up the aisle, I see that my mother is also standing at the altar. She notices me seconds later and smiles. With tears in her eyes, she lovingly reaches out to me. I hesitate, because I can't recall the last time I'd received a hug from her. Not knowing what to expect, I open my arms to receive her embrace. In that moment, years of pain were forgiven and a new beginning started. Mother hugged me for what seemed like an eternity and for the first time in years, called me Cynthia.

The End.

Lareesa Fonville Willis

The End.

Note from Author

Thank you for taking the time to read my first book! I bless God for giving me the imagination and the talent to be able to become an author. These gifts have been inside me for years, but somehow fear stood in my way of sharing my writings. I was scared of how I might be perceived if certain subjects were brought up, if I wrote in a particular style, etc. Nobody wants to be judged. But, with age comes wisdom and I've learned that it's not about what people think. It's solely about what God thinks. He has given me permission and the courage to share a bit of myself with the world. This "quiet girl" has a lot to say, so look out! This is only the beginning of what you will hear and see from me. Please keep me in your prayers as I strive to do His will.

Feel free to contact me with any questions, feedback, reviews, or book inquiries. I can be reached via email at lareesainc@aol.com, online channels at @lareesainc, or by mail at:

Cyn No More Book
P. O. Box 35893
Richmond, VA 23235

I look forward to hearing from you.

Love and hugs,
Lareesa

Lareesa Fonville Willis